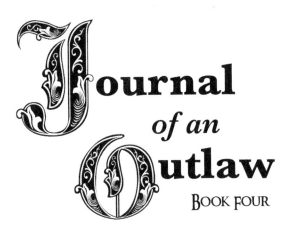

Journal of an Outlaw

BOOK FOUR

THE LONGEST TALE

Written by Mick McArt
Cover Art by Matthew McEntire

MICK ART
PRODUCTIONS LLC
PUBLISHING
WWW.MICKARTPRODUCTIONS.COM

Journal of an Outlaw, Book 4 "The Longest Tale"
All Rights Reserved
Copyright © 2021 Mick McArt, Mick Art Productions
V1

ISBN: 978-1-948508-09-4

Published by
Mick Art Productions, LLC
www.mickartproductions.com

PRINTED IN THE UNITED STATES OF AMERICA

THIS BOOK IS DEDICATED
TO CHASING TREASURE,
WHETHER IT BE OF
THE HEART OR THROUGH
THE WRITTEN WORD.

Reviews from the Realms

"I was blown away!"
- Bernie Wixx, Gunpowder Press

"Each chapter gave me the chills."
- A.W. Frosty, The Cold Times

"I absorbed the whole book ... and it's reader!"
- Jelly Cube, random dungeon

"It looks great! I promise to read it tomorrow."
- Gunner Chekidout, Daily Procrastinator

"I swear I might have read this before."
- Bendare Dunndat, Deja News

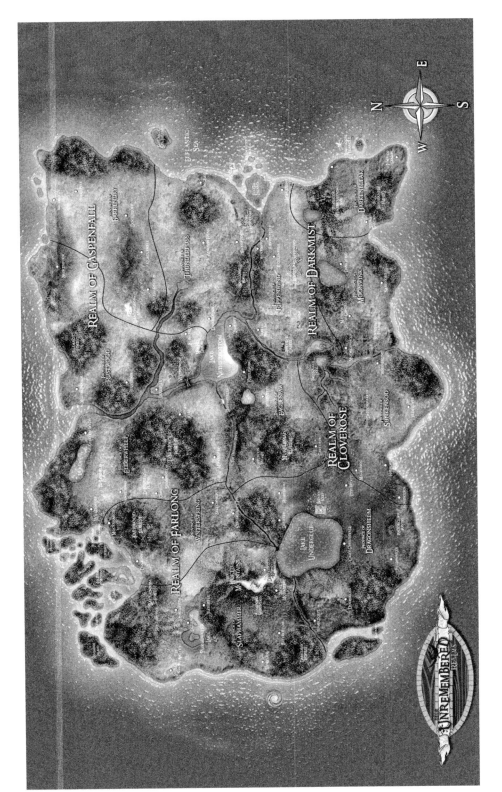

Thank You's

God; Erica McArt; my children Micah, Jonah, & Emerald; Matthew McEntire for the amazing cover art and giving the Unremembered Realms a great visual identity; Marilyn McArt; Curt "Spaceburt' Coker; Kristen Coker; Chuck Bailey; Mickey McArt; Randy Pearson; Dave Wehner; the Bila family; The Amazin' Mitten; Bruce Shields; Dave Robishaw; Eric Allison; Andy Schiller; Tom Vasel; Eric Summerer; Justin Andrew Mason; Martin Kealey; Luke Gygax; Donato Giancola; Rusty Myers, and last but not least Jennifer Bouchard who proofs all my wacky attempts at writing proper english!

Mick Art Productions Publishing
www.theunrememberedrealms.com

Journal of an Outlaw - Book 4 "The Longest Tale"
Written by Mick McArt
Cover Art by Matt McEntire
Map by Justin Andrew Mason
Editing by Jennifer Bouchard
Story consistancy checking by Erica McArt
and extra editing by Micah McArt

Chapter 1

I stood under the wooden sign that hung over the front of the Palm Eye Finger Magic Shop. The sun was settling over the city of Neverspring, and I was looking forward to a peaceful night of security. The shop owners, Bub and Lar, had paid me to keep an eye on the place while they went with their wives on vacation to Port Laudervale. I didn't mind the job, the two elderly wizards had been good to me throughout my life, and it was the least I could do to help them.

Bub and Lar had set up a whole slew of security measures before handing me the key and taking off. There were multiple magical traps waiting for any nogoodnik who might get any funny ideas about robbing the place. Not only that, but a rival magic shop called Schmendrake's had opened across the street, and the two wizards didn't like the looks of its owner. Schmendrake was a balding, middle-aged human magic-user with thick horn-rimmed glasses who despised the two wizards. He wasn't nearly as powerful and the items in his store were nowhere near the high-quality goods that are sold at the Palm Eye Finger Magic Shop.

The two wizards were worried that the lesser mage would use any opportunity to get the upper hand on them. I told them not to worry and to go on their trip. I had faith in their setup, and I would be watching the place like a hawk. Reassured, the duo and their wives waved goodbye and stepped through a teleportation portal they had created.

I was finally alone on the quiet street. Most of the other shops had closed, and only a few other people would pass, occasionally, on their way home or to a local tavern. I walked around the shop before going back to the front door and doing a few stretches to stay limber. The night was only beginning, and I was sure the rougher crowd would be out soon. I knew this, because I was one of them!

Staying up all night never bothered me; I hardly slept. Even when I did, it was mostly during the day, unless I was traveling with a regular-hours party. I preferred the chill of a nightly breeze to the simmering rays of the sun. Light tended to expose any picking of pockets, which was a favored sport of mine.

There was hardly any noise at the moment; just the creak of the wooden sign hanging on its rusty metal chain and the small "ting" that my favorite gold coin made as I flipped it up in the air out of boredom. I liked seeing the golden circle as it rotated in the air. It always seemed to calm me. It was an older coin, with lots of dings and smudges all over it. It also happened to be magical. It was called the Coin of Cheating, which meant it landed on whichever side the owner wanted. I acquired it from a band of ruffian dwarves known as the Black Willows. Their leader, Quade, was in love with it and was on a quest to get it back... at any cost.

The coin had the King of Cloverose on one side and a gem embossed on the other. I often wondered where this coin had been in its travels. Coins always fascinated me. They could be in the hand of a man one moment, then in a claw of a dragon the next, and then back, again. I wondered how much blood had been spilled over its acquisition. It didn't matter though, it was mine now, and things seemed to be peaceful for me, at this juncture in life.

"Bored, thief?" a figure asked as it walked up to me.

It was Schmendrake. His smirk was from ear-to-ear. "Because the night is young," he continued. "And I spotted some rich couples strolling in front of a tavern a few streets down."

"For one thing, magician," I began. "I'm not a thief; I'm a rogue. There's a difference. I'm here guarding the store against low-level thugs, such as yourself."

Schmendrake kept smiling, even though I noticed his brow furrowed. He pulled out a small stack of coins and gave them a quick jingle. "You know, rogue," he said with disdain. "It could benefit both of us if you came to work for me. I have gold, jewels, and even a few magic items, like Boots of Jumping. You'd like those."

"I don't think so," I said, giving the coin another flip and catching it. "I'm content right here."

"Nice coin," Schmedrake said. "It looks rare."

"I wouldn't admire too much," I said, brushing away a flap of

2

my cloak, revealing my deadly magical dagger, Magurk. "Staring too long can give people sharp, stabbing pains all over their bodies."

"Hmph," Schmendrake replied, taking a step back. "I'm warning you. The Palm Eye Finger Magic Shop won't be open much longer, once my shop takes off. Then you'll be sorry you ever worked with those two geezers!"

I stepped forward two steps and caused the wizard to turn and run a few feet. "Aaah," he shrieked. "Stay away from me!"

"Scram, you scruff," I said, chuckling. "Or I might come shopping at your store later. After hours, of course!"

Schmendrake ran a few more paces, then turned around and mumbled something before pointing a finger in my direction. A flash of green light went off and nearly blinded me, for a second. I checked myself over, but nothing seemed out of sorts. My blood was boiling at the thought of this dimwit casting something at me.

"Curse you and your stupid coin!" he yelled while running away. "You haven't seen the last of me!"

I grabbed the Swatfly Bow off my back and notched an arrow, but the wizard disappeared in a magical puff of smoke. "Cheap parlor trick," I said to myself, placing my bow back into its place.

Within five minutes, I was leaning on the door, again, flipping my coin and humming a song I had heard at the Sidebucket Tavern. As I flipped the coin, I heard a scream for help that disrupted my thoughts. Startled, I missed the coin. It bounced on the ground and began rolling away from me and down the road. I never miss catching a coin flip, I thought to myself as I quickly started to chase it. Something seemed odd.

As I ran, I noticed a dark figure running my way from the opposite direction. He was carrying a coin purse that he had obviously just stolen, since he was running away from an overweight elven woman who was yelling after him. I would have let him go, but I noticed that he had spotted my rolling coin and lowered his hand to the ground to snatch it up.

I tackled him, head-on, knocking the wind from him. He wasn't expecting that I could run so fast, but I had my magical Boots of Speeding, and we connected with quite an impact. The elven lady

3

pounded on the stunned fool, while I secretly lifted her coin purse, before I jumped back up, trying to locate my runaway coin. I spotted a moonlight flash off of it and took off. Much to my chagrin, by the time I reached for it, the coin fell through the bars of a sewer grate.

"No!" I yelled out in frustration.

I placed my ear the grate and I could hear it clink on something, and then spin a little, and then the sound of it continuing to roll. When I pushed myself back up, I noticed the grate was loose, so I grabbed the rusty metal bars and gave it a small tug. It worked! The round grate came out easily, so I sat it down next to a pile of spilled trash. A small rat scurried out of the garbage and curiously blinked at me.

"What," I stated, addressing the smelly rodent. "That's my favorite coin!"

The rat squeaked and ran off as I slung my legs over the lip of the hole. I felt around with my feet until I found a metal ladder leading downward. I slipped the grate back over my head just in time as the overweight elf lady, who must have realized that she had been robbed, yet again, stepped over it. "I'll kill you if I ever find you, thief!" she yelled out into the empty street.

If I had a copper for every time I heard that, I could give up being a rogue and retire! While she stood there yelling out threats, I climbed down the ladder and leaped off the last rung. It was a big mistake. My feet made a splash in the watery liquid that covered the floor. I cringed and looked up, only to see the face of the elf staring down through the grate directly at me! "I can see your green eye, rogue! You're dead meat!"

Sometimes I forget that my right eye, which was replaced by a lich's, lightly glowed green. Sure, this eye came in handy for seeing in the dark, but it also made me stick out like a sore thumb in situations like this! I watched as she removed the grate and tried to climb down, only to get stuck. "Someone get me some grease!" she yelled. "Help!"

"You should have ate before you went out for the night," I yelled up at her.

"I never forget a face, I will find you!" she huffed and puffed.

I saw this as my cue to exit and chase my missing coin. After a quick inspection of the area, I noticed a small misplacement of slime on a waist-high ledge. It had a small line that led away from me down deeper into the sewer tunnel. I started my journey to the sound of the frustrated elf cursing me and breaking wind. Wherever this tunnel led me, I did not want to come back in this direction!

Chapter 2

Thanks to my lich eye, I was able to follow the ledge for quite a ways. Sometimes, I wanted to strangle Fumblegums the Cleric for putting this eye in me, and other times, only slightly strangle him, because it has helped me on many occasions. The mumbling healer was lucky he had healed me of so many other horrific wounds on other occasions.

Making my way through the city sewers was not a pleasant experience. Not only was the odor terrible, but I thought I could hear the occasional flush of someone's victory over their bowels. I dreaded being in places like this. I'd take the dangers of roguery one thousand times over switching places with a plumber. To make it to the top in that business, you have to go straight to the bottom!

I had only been following the trail a few minutes when I noticed some writing in chalk above the ledge where my coin's trail had stopped. There was a finger smudge in the slime so I knew someone had snagged it and ran off. There was also a piece of chalk. That's when I figured out that whoever wrote on the wall, had just stolen my coin. I figured this graffiti might be the only clue I would get, so I tried to decipher the weird mix of orc and common:

It read:

"In droppings deep, the fume arises
No one suspects our foul surprises
Meet us under the temple for poetic justice
From those above who privily shunned us."

5

I had no idea what any of this meant, but I figured with poetry this bad, they must be a starving artist and needed the coin for food. I figured that this person must be truly bizarre. I mean, who hangs in the city waste tunnels and writes poetry about it? I hoped they weren't going to put up much of a fight over my coin; just the thought of getting in physical combat with someone covered in who-knows-what gave me the shivers. It was bad enough that my boots were getting dirty in this mess!

I was sure which way to go, but then I noticed a hand-shaped wipe on a tunnel wall. They had wiped the sludge off their hand after picking up the coin! I marched through the ankle-deep sludge as quietly as I could in that direction, occasionally passing small rats, here and there. The smell grew worse the farther I went. It re-minded me of a druid before their annual mudbath! It could be worse, though; that overweight elf lady could have sat on me and yelled for local authorities. I've been locked up in many prisons, but the nasty one in Neverspring made this sewer seem like the Cloverose Palace!

As I walked on, I pondered over the words 'privily shunned us'. It made it sound as if the person I was looking for was part of a group. The poet also mentioned a meeting under the temple. That was a good clue, because I had a pretty good sense of location, and I knew that the Temple of Gallowman was not that far away from the Palm Eye Finger Magic Shop. Healy, my main party's cleric, had dropped into this quiet temple to hear lectures and talk shop with other healers. If I had to guess, I'd say the clerics in the temple had made an enemy and were probably going to be under siege, at some point.

My directional instincts had proven correct, because as I moved forward to where I thought the temple might be, I heard the distinct sound of fingers making snapping noises. That's also when I listened to another poem as it was shouted out:

"*From the bottom, we'll erupt*
and plunge the foul waters of the corrupt
pushing out from cisternic cellars
together we'll conquer above ground dwellers!"

It was a female's voice with some weird accent, which did not sound entirely human. That's when I noticed a bit of light in the corridor up ahead. I cautiously crept forward and could see that there was an open archway. I quietly walked up to it and peeked through. The room was large and filled with about a hundred or so people, consisting of dirty looking humanoids of every race, class, and living status. By living status, I mean undead. There was quite a lot of them, especially zombies, sitting on long rows of benches, with their arms held firmly over their heads and fingers ready to snap.

There was a coffee-making station in the back with multiple tenders and patrons going back and forth; the ones that were alive, anyway. I shuddered at the thought of sewer coffee. Something told me it probably tasted like crap. Up in the front was a stage with large velvety red curtains pulled aside. Standing there, wearing a brown beret, was the speaker I must have been hearing. She was an oddly attractive half-orc female with sloppy makeup and horrible hair done up in the latest style (that I had accidentally made famous when visiting the Queen of Cloverose).

The woman ranted and raved, moving about the stage all herky-jerky, trying to be entertaining, and inspirational. Fingers were snapping in affirmation to whatever nonsense she was spewing when I noticed a flyer hanging on the entrance wall. I quietly reached over and grabbed it when everyone else was preoccupied.

It read "Tonight! Come hear our glorious leader, Bjorc, as she prepares us!" Then, there were big letters below with a copyrighted logo that read 'Undead Poet's Society.' In even larger letters below that were the words "B.Y.O.W. (Bring Your Own Weapons)."

They must be planning to attack the temple tonight, I thought to myself. The war-mongering poets would probably organize a surprise attack on the peaceful temple above. I surmised that with most of the healers gone, this group would overflow into the city, fouling up everything. It was good for an evil plan, but from the looks of these nitwits, I didn't think they'd get too far before Red Eye Knights or even the Gallowman clerics flush these jokers down the drain. I didn't want to get involved; I just wanted my coin back.

I didn't know what fool in this place had it.

"This is a sign!" Bjorc yelled out from the stage, holding up her light green hand.

In between her thumb and finger was my golden Coin of Cheating! The audience ooo'd and ahhh'd while she held it up, pacing back and forth on stage, making sure all could see. "This has been enchanted with powerful magic," she declared. "This shall be a symbol of what's coming, and how we, against all odds, will rise and flood the streets, clogging the back end of Neverspring!"

The audience started snapping like crazy and clinking their coffee mugs together in agreement. That's the moment I saw one of the coffee tenders walk out from behind the counter and head to what looked like a latrine door. Using my Blending Cloak, I quietly slipped in behind him. Moments later, I reappeared from the lavatory, using my Hat of Disguise, and the unconscious tender's cloak, to move back behind the counter.

While other servers were distracted with pouring coffee for attendees, I quickly removed the filter screen and hid it in my cloak. Knowing I had little time, I ran from behind the counter and made my way to the stage. I took off my Hat of Disguise and shouted, "You call those rhymes?!" at Bjorc. "Why don't you let a real poet up there?"

The room instantly hushed, well, except for the zombies, who just groaned a bit between drools. The poetess looked at me with a stunned expression. "What? Who? How dare you challenge me!" she began, "I am the leader of Rise from the Bottom! Guards! Don't let this man cause a stir!"

A few armored zombies wearing berets appeared from the multitude of people, but I jumped up on the stage before they could reach me. "What is that I smell?" I yelled out to the crowd while pinching my nose.

Obvious answers were shouted back, but then I interrupted, "Fear! It's a foul thing to come from a leader, and Bjorc's is extra whiffy!"

The crowd roared and jumped to their feet, shouting up to the stage, causing Bjorc to step back. She held up her hands and signaled for silence. She shot me a menacing look, then spoke. "All right then, stranger, challenge accepted, Mr. um, what is your name?"

"Brown water," I lied, thinking about coffee. "Maxwell Brownwater"

"So, Maxwell," Bjorc hissed, approaching me. "The house is yours…for a moment!"

Using her index finger, she poked me in the chest, trying to intimidate me. Not wanting to miss an opportunity, I used my minor telekinesis power to take back my coin and put the coffee screen into her robes. Bjorc was so angry at that moment; she didn't even notice the exchange. The excitement of having my coin back made me smile. "You won't be smiling long, Brownwater," Bjorc hissed at me between clenched teeth.

"I figured that," I whispered back. "I have to hear more of your dumb poetry."

I walked to the middle of the stage, pulled back my hood, and took a moment to clear my throat. Raising an open palm at the ceiling, I began to make up a bunch of nonsense, which any goofball could tell was complete pap.

"Cleansing is a necessity, if changes are to occur,
for when they point their fingers above us, we'll pull them for sure
everyone up there, from the largest to the minuscule
will fear what they find when we've entered their pool
we'll wipe them all out, in homes or caves
and they'll fertilize flowers from their graves!"

The crowd cheered and began snapping their fingers like crazy. I smiled and did a slight bow, shooting a glance over at Bjorc, who was now fuming! Her patience must have worn off, because she placed her hand on the hilt of the shortsword that she had strapped to her belt and started coming for me. Then, there was a scream! Everyone froze as a voice cried out, "Someone has stolen the coffee filter! There's no more coffee without it! What will we do?!"

The entire crowd turned to the stage, hoping for an answer from Bjorc. "If something's been stolen, it's easy to tell who took it; Maxwell Brownwater is even dressed like a thief! Here, let me prove it!"

As she got closer to me, she withdrew her sword from its sheath. Once again I used my telekinesis power and pulled the small screen from her pocket. It fell to the floor, where it rolled to the front of the stage! The crowd hushed for only a moment before breaking out in a huge roar! "Fakir!" someone screamed out at Bjorc, "She wasn't a poet, and we didn't know it!"

I slowly retreated to the back of the stage after shouting, "She was after our coffee the whole time!"

Ducking behind a curtain, I found a ladder that rose about thirty feet to the ceiling and began to climb. At the top was a manhole cover that was perforated with coin-sized holes. I gently lifted it open and climbed out. Once I got up, I could see that I was in a large abandoned kitchen. The manhole was the drain they used in their day-to-day mop-up operations of Gallowman Temple, of which I now assumed I was in.

The kitchen smelled wonderfully of food, and there was lots of it set out all over multiple counters. I wondered if there was a feast going on. I ran over to a sink, washed my hands, and grabbed a hot loaf of bread. I took a few bites before realizing that I better put the manhole cover back. I sat the snack down and walked back over, peering down the hole.

"There he is!" came Bjorc's voice from below, "he tricked us and stole our coin!"

I could see her beat-up face, and she did not look happy. A crowd of her sewer dwellers climbed the ladder, so I shoved the manhole cover back into place. I glanced around, found a heavy-looking cauldron, and got around it, pushing it with my back toward the hole. It was just over the top of it when I heard the banging of the angry poets below. I knew I had to get out of there, and fast, so I started to run using my Boots of Speeding.

I flew out the door and through the mess hall, which was also abandoned. Then, I ran down two twisty corridors and through some offices. I didn't know where all the clerics were, at this point, and I didn't care. I just had to get out of there.

Chapter 3

While running through Gallowman Temple, I grabbed the coin from my pocket, held it up between my index finger and thumb, and smiled. It felt good to have it back. I couldn't wait to use it again at the Dice Tower Tavern. It always felt fantastic cheating some sap out of their money, especially if they were part of some nasty gang or mob-connected. I always loved the dumbfounded look on their faces when, no matter how many times the coin would flip, it was always in my favor. It usually ended up in some tavern brawl, which I didn't mind. That meant knocked out teeth, and some would be gold!

I should have known not to be distracted while running this magically fast, because anything could have happened, and it did! Through an ornate door, I passed a small waiting room and tripped over a travel pack that was left near some large curtains.

I am an excellent tumbler, but due to my enhanced speed, I was caught off guard and ended up landing on my chest and sliding on the polished marble floor. I slid through some huge curtains and came to a halt in a brightly lit auditorium filled with hundreds of people! I stopped sliding to the gasp of the crowd. "Amazing!" came a voice from just next to me.

A hand reached down, taking my coin from between my fingers. "Here is someone with such a heart of giving that they nearly hurt themselves trying to tithe!"

I looked around the room to the now applauding audience of clerics. I realized that it was a special event that I had slid into. I gave them a small grin and a wave after I rose to my feet. I watched in horror as the cleric who had spoken dropped my coin into a collection basket next to the podium.

"Has anyone here ever seen such a heart of charity?" the speaker asked the audience as their applause died down. "Now, if you'll have a seat, sir, we will resume our all-night lecture on the benefits of powdered acorn caps and their ability to get rid of the side effects of healing broths."

Not knowing what to do, but not wanting to abandon my coin, I went to the only space open on the pew in the front row. It was between two chubby dwarven clerics, who repeatedly muttered across me to each other, commenting on what must be the realm's most boring lecture. As they leaned together, they would crush me. Their breath smelled like they ate socks for dinner and washed them down with ogre sweat. After five minutes of this, I decided to slide from my seat to the floor and crawled toward the basket. Maybe no one would pay attention, and I could slip away unnoticed with the coin!

Before I could get a few feet, I heard my nickname yelled out. "Gwai Lo!" said a voice, loudly. "Ith me! Fumblegumth!"

While I was making my move, the head cleric had introduced their guest speaker, who happened to be a quirky traveling companion of mine, Fumblegums the Cleric. He was the one responsible for me having a lizardman hand and a lich eye. The cleric was as annoying as he was useful, and his speech impediment made him stand out in every situation. "I'm the getht thpeaker tonight, ithunt that great?!"

I immediately flashed back to when I tripped and remembered the travel pack; it was the old toothless cleric's! I immediately turned red in anger. "Remind me to have a special talk with you later," I said, standing up and cracking my knuckles.

"Thure!" Fumblegums responded with a big grin, "Ecthullent!"

I slunk back to the pew, feeling defeated and more frustrated than ever. The chubby dwarves lifted their fat rolls on either side, so I could slip between them. It was gross, but warm. I swear I could feel their sweaty dampness even through my clothing and cloak! Fumblegums began his lecture by lifting his arm and pointing to the skin on it. "Epidermith!" he stated.

"Epidermith," the audience repeated, not knowing he had a lisp from his lack of teeth.

I rolled my eyes and began looking around for a way to escape. The minute they were distracted, I planned on grabbing the basket and making a break for it. I didn't care at that point how many lightning spells they called down from the clouds at me.

The two dwarves muttered across from me about clericky things that I didn't understand, then passed a sack full of fried potato crisps back and forth to one another. The crumbs did not only end up in their beards, but all over me, as well. They offered me some, but I just shook my head. The cleric behind me kept coughing, too, and it was starting to get on my nerves. I mean, weren't all these people clerics? Heal yourself, for realm's sake!

At this point, Fumblegums waved back toward the curtain behind him. A skeleton emerged and walked to the front of the platform. The kooky cleric began pointing to certain bones and discussing mending techniques. I used this as my opportunity to make a move.

I stood up and yelled, "It's hiding something; look out!"

I ran to the platform and tackled the skeleton, knocking it to the ground. The crowd in the room gasped as I pretended to choke the animated creature. "What are you doing?" Fumblegums asked, standing over me.

It was apparent that none of them believed me. As I stood up from the motionless skeleton, I could see the rows of frowning faces. "False alarm, nothing to see here," I said as I held up my hands.

"Why do you thmell like dwarf thwet?" Fumblegums asked, in a low tone.

Before I could make up an answer, there came a cry from behind the large stage curtains. "There's the thief!"

I could see the swollen face of Bjorc as she screamed and ran toward me. A sizable number of her sewer dwellers followed her. The clerics wasted no time meeting this threat head-on. As weapons clashed and spells lit up the room, I dove for the collection basket and slid on the floor, dodging a cultist's sword and snagging it. With my prize in the basket, I ran for the exit. None of the clerics or cultists stood in my way, so I ran top speed, never looking back or slowing my pace.

The door quickly flung open when I pushed it, and I flew out. In my haste, I did not see the halfling who was walking in the shadows. I tripped over him, causing both of us to sprawl on the ground! The basket flew from my hands and its contents flew into the air before scattering all over the cobblestones like golden confetti. The squeaky voice of the halfling yelled out, "Watch where you are going, fool!"

A few locals had appeared as if from out of nowhere, excitedly retrieving the spilled gold coinage. "Stop! Thieves!" I cried, standing back up to try to stop them as they hurriedly scooped as many coins as they could.

"Look what I found," a familiar voice said as I looked up. "A free gold coin!"

A large human male held my magical coin up to the moonlight and admired the sparkle. The figure was none other than Onquay, a fellow Crimson Roof Thieves Guild rogue and dim-witted nemesis of mine. "I hope this was yours," he said to me before kicking me in the chest with his boot and sending me flying backward.

I flew helplessly back into the halfling, knocking him over, once again. "My maps!" he cried out as bits of parchment flew all around.

After a quick cough, I looked up, only to see Onquay disappearing around a corner about a block away. "Gwai Lo, you clumsy oaf!" the halfling muttered as he gathered his wits about him. "I better not be missing one of these treasure maps. They are priceless!"

It was Robbie the Thief, another guild member who wasn't on my good list. "You're the one who ruined my escape!" I said, pointing at the door.

You could hear the sounds of battle coming from inside the temple and see an occasional flash from a spell going off. "Thanks to you, I lost something special to that oversized lame brain! Now, I'll have to track him down, and that could take all night!"

Robbie just smiled. "I know where he went," he stated, while holding up his hand and rubbing two fingers together against his thumb. "What's it worth to you?"

I did not hesitate and started strangling the little crud. "You..reek...of...dwarf...sweat...and...sewage!" he gasped.

I tightened my grip until he gave me the information I needed.

"They…are…in…the …back of…the old Delappador apartment building," he managed to gasp out. "They've been holed up there awaiting orders from their boss. Elfalfuh."

I should have finished strangling him, but I was in a hurry, so I dropped the gasping worm and took off in Onquay's direction. I smiled as I ran, because the twerp didn't notice the small bag of coins I took from him!

Chapter 4

When I got to the alley and looked down, it didn't appear promising. Door after door lined the alleyway where businesses left discarded boxes and trash bins. I quickly and quietly checked a few door handles as I made my way. Even if I could get inside, there was no guarantee that I would find Onquay. He was probably hidden away with Apichat, his partner in crime, behind a secret door cooking up some nefarious plot to get rich. These two bottom dwellers had no respect for anything. Their overconfidence in their own abilities was their weak spot, so I just had to figure out how to get to them and exploit it. Just the thought of robbing them blind and possibly giving them both a swift kick to the backside made me happy. There was nothing I enjoyed more than wiping the smug look off their faces.

"Which door could it possibly be?" I whispered to myself as I walked further down. "Maybe the dimwits actually listened to their teachers at the guild about hiding out and…"

Before I could finish my thought, I saw a crudely written note stuck to a door that read, 'We are here.' "Somehow, I am not surprised," I mumbled as I walked up to it. "How dumb can they…"

"Excuse me, mister," a voice cried out from the alley opening. "Excuse me!"

When I looked over, I saw a pimply elfling delivery boy holding a bag of food. "I'm looking for a Mr. Onquay. He said he'd leave a note on the door."

I quickly pulled the note down and smiled as the kid ap-

15

proached. He wore a grease-stained tunic and a hat that had "Mud-flow Tavern" embroidered on it. "That's me," I told the teen. "I'm Mr. Onquay."

I took out Robbie's coin purse, paid for the food, and gave a generous tip. "Thanks, Mr. Onquay," the elfling smiled. "I had heard you never tip. Just wait until I tell the guys!"

I watched him scamper off, then I sat the food bag down and reached into my backpack for my magical Hat of Disguising. I un-crumpled it, pulled my hood back, then placed it carefully on my head. Within the blink of an eye, my appearance was transformed into that of the greasy elfling kid. I loved my magical hat; I can't tell you how many times it has gotten me out of bad situations.

When I knelt to open the food bag, I removed a vial from the potion bandolier that I wore across my chest and gave it a quick shake. It was a Flying Bull potion; another one of my favorite things to get me out of a jam. It usually played havoc on the intes-tines, if you know what I mean. I reached into the bag, took out their sandwiches, and soaked both of them with the odorless liq-uid. I chuckled to myself, knowing things wouldn't be odorless for long! After placing the food back in the bag, I reclosed it and stood up before giving the door a knock.

I could hear talking from behind the door as they got closer. "You should have stabbed him, Onquay," a familiar voice spoke.

"I didn't want to miss our order," Onquay's voice replied. "I'm starving."

I could hear a few bolts slide open, and then the door. "You're late, kid. No tip!"

Onquay grabbed the bag and handed me a few coins, none of which was my magic one, and he went to slam the door. "That's okay," I replied, patting Robbie's stolen coin purse. "Other people have been very generous tonight."

Onquay raised an eyebrow. "I see," he said. "You ever gamble, kid?"

"Not really," I lied. "But I used to beat my cousin Hoyle at Old Maiden."

"C'mon in, then," he said, smiling. "Appy and I were getting bored, anyway."

It wasn't long before the three of us were sitting around the table, staring at our cards. I could feel the breeze from the street through an open window behind me. I could also see the battle between the clerics and the poets as it grew more intense from this position. Apichat and Onquay both laughed as they saw a human cleric fall to the ground and die, just across the street.

I had forgotten how much being around these two annoyed me. It almost made me wish I was still stuck between the two obese dwarves listening to that boring lecture by Fumblegums. Apichat had a bad habit of licking his sandwich before each bite like he was torturing it or something. Onquay, on the other hand, ate his food without hesitation, leaving dark sauce around his mouth, making him resemble a demented clown; which, seemed appropriate to me, since that's what he was.

By the third hand of cards, I figured my plan was about to take course. I've seen Flying Bull work its way through a dragon before, so I knew these two clods wouldn't be sitting here much longer. I had two pairs and felt confident that if the potion hadn't started to kick in, at least I'd be making some good coin. I put my ante up into the coin pile in the center of the table and called the hand. Both of Elfalfuh's henchmen smiled and added their coins, as well. To my delight, I could see my coin as Onquay tossed it in. "Nice coin," Apichat commented as he picked it up. "I swear I've seen this before…"

Before he could finish his sentence, Apichat expelled a loud bit of gas. "Whoa," Onquay laughed. "That's the smartest thing you've said all day!"

"Something's not right," Apichat said, putting his hand over his stomach, dropping my coin back into the pile. "I think we've been poisoned!"

"What!?" Onquay yelled, flipping the table over in a fit of rage.

Cards and coins flew everywhere. I was knocked backward off my chair and watched helplessly as my coin flew above me, just out of my grasp, and out the partially opened window. Apichat grabbed a chair and was about to strike me with it, then doubled

17

over after another disturbing noise. "My new trousers!" he yelled before running down a hallway leading away from us.

Onquay, on the other hand, wasn't affected, just yet. He grabbed me off the floor by my throat with both hands and lifted me in the air. But, before he could smash me, I managed to jam both my thumbs into his eyes and kick off his chest. Through the force of my kick and him throwing me off, I was hurled through the window, breaking it and flying out onto the street! I could feel bits of glass stuck in my back and warm blood running down. My Hat of Disguising had fallen off, so I grabbed it quickly, but apparently, not fast enough.

"You!" The big rogue yelled at me through the broken window, rubbing his eyes. "You must have been in cahoots with that delivery boy! I'm going to kill you, ghost man!"

The pale-eyed maniac broke wind and stopped shaking his fist. "Oh, no," he muttered before disappearing back into the house.

I frantically began to search for my coin. I realized this wasn't going to be easy, because by this time, the whole area had broken into an all-out brawl between the clerics and the Undead Poet Society. They had filled the street and it was now a full-blown riot!

Luckily, I spotted the magical glow from my coin, once more, and saw it rolling down the road. Disregarding my pain, I got up and started to run toward it. I tucked my Hat of Disguising into a hidden pocket of my cloak, before jumping over a couple of bodies with the full intention of getting my prize back. Then, I heard a voice cry out, "Gwai Lo!"

When I looked down, I could see the battered body of Fumblegums the Cleric. He was in rough shape, but he still managed a toothless grin. "Thank goodneth you're here," he groaned, holding his side. "You can help me!"

I looked at the coin rolling farther away, then back at the goofy looking Cleric. I started to take a step for the coin, but ultimately stopped and sighed, letting my head fall. "What can I do?" I said, defeatedly.

"I have a healing pothan in my pack," he replied. "I can't reath it."

I leaned him forward and opened his pack. I pulled out a ball of yarn, a jar labeled "gum cleaner," a half-eaten sandwich, and three unmatched socks. "Really?" I said, showing them to him.

"You never know," he coughed. "I could thtill find the matcheth."

I reached deeper into the pack and felt something slimy. I closed my eyes, moved past it, and found the Healing Potion. I pulled it out, uncorked it with my teeth, and spit out the cork. I gave it a quick sip before pouring the contents into the bumbling cleric's mouth. I could feel my back wounds heal slightly as I watched Fumblegums side wound heal up. "What a day," the Cleric stated. "Thankth, Gwai Lo, I just want to thay…"

Those were the last words I heard, because I was already off and running in the direction of my lost Coin of Cheating. It was hard to see anything in the street due to the ongoing battle between the clerics and the undead zealot forces, but to my amazement, I spotted it. Dead center in the middle of the fight was Fumblegum's demonstration skeleton that he had raised. It stood there moving its head around like it was looking for something. Stuck between two of its toe bones was my coin!

I started ducking and dodging blows as I made my way to the animated creature. My wide growing grin of hope did not last long, though, because I heard a familiar female voice ring out. "You!" she shrieked. "You ruined all of our plans!"

When I turned around, I could see Bjorc standing there with a prepped lightning spell coursing between her long green fingers. "I don't know how you did it, rogue, infiltrating our base and botching up our secret plans. But all that doesn't matter now; I'm going to fry you dead!"

I braced for the blast as she raised her hands, but then, out of the blue, the two overweight dwarves I sat between earlier came out of nowhere at full speed and crushed her between them! Bjorc let out a loud grunt before collapsing on the ground, groaning. "Well, thanks," I said, in surprise.

"Anything for a pew mate," the one said as they both laughed. "Now, let's give this scumbagette a good ole fashioned hurl!"

Both dwarves picked her up, then, on the count of three, hurled her over my head. As I watched her fall, I realized it was precisely where the skeleton was standing. Bjorc hit the creature with such an impact that the bones exploded in every direction! All except the foot, which stayed right where it was with my coin. "Phew," I muttered.

But as I started to make my way over, a dog ran out of nowhere, snatched the foot from its place, and ran off down the street. This wasn't just any dog, though, it was Iris, the one-eyed bulldog that belonged to Previn Dukes, the overpriced Cleric who treated me once-in-a-while. "Iris, come back!" I shouted, hearing Previn call the same thing at the same time.

We both ran after the dog, but for very different reasons.

Chapter 5

"What are you doing here, Previn?" I panted as we made our way through the battle.

"I was here to hear the lecture by Fumblegums. I've admired him for years!" Previn explained. "Isn't he the best?"

I've got to make better acquaintances, I thought to myself. "Your dog is fast," I huffed, "Iris must have really wanted that bone!"

Previn laughed as we ran. Then, I asked, "Didn't you ever teach your mutt how to fetch?"

"Only the first half," the cleric replied. "I guess I was too busy healing people coming into my clinic every other day for injuries they got from taking things that didn't belong to them!"

I had a pithy response to the accusation, but I lost my train of thought when I saw Iris leave the battle, run off the road, and enter a cornfield. "That's just great," I yelled, stopping at the edge, panting. "Now, what do we do?"

"We'll spread six feet apart and move forward," Previn replied. "If I know Iris, he'll stop for a quick chew, then move on. Perhaps we can surround him and snag him up before he runs off, again.

It sounded reasonable. But even if it didn't, what choice did I have? I just hoped the coin was still stuck in the skeleton's foot. Not only that, but when I looked back toward the battle, I could see Apichat and Onquay worming their way through the crowd in our direction. I didn't think they had spotted me, yet, so I quickly made my way into the tall cornstalks. Usually, I could handle these two nitwits, but I didn't want to lose track of my coin.

After about ten minutes of walking and searching, Previn found a piece of a toe bone. "It's got a bite mark on it," he noted from a couple of rows across.

"See anything else? Like a unique gold coin?" I asked.

"No, sir," he replied. "But I'm confident Iris will be tiring out, soon. All this battle stuff is a lot of excitement for him!"

We both moved forward, again. I was glad for such a bright full moon; hopefully, I'd catch a glimmer off of my circular prize. The cornfield ended not much farther along, and we realized we were at the edge of a forest. With a silent nod, we both entered. Both of us knew the dangers of entering a forest at night in the Unremembered Realms. So, we didn't make the decision lightly. There were so many dangerous creatures that thrived in our world, that someone had compiled a book called the Manual of Monsters to keep track of them. Years after that informative publication, came the follow-up, called the Folio of Fiends. I swear I had run into every creature in it, but the Unremembered Realms is so vast that it never surprised me when I ran into something new.

Today was no exception. Previn and I had not been in the woods very long when we heard Iris growling. "That doesn't sound good," the cleric whispered. "Iris must feel threatened."

We both crept forward, slowly, and soon laid eyes on the dog, the skeleton foot, and luckily, my coin! The problem was that the dog was surrounded by a half-dozen creatures that I did not recognize. "Morelleons," Previn whispered. "Living mushrooms."

The animated plant creatures appeared to be about five feet in height, had thick stem bodies, and weird, elongated caps for heads. I would have laughed at how they appeared, except they had sharp looking claws extending out from their upper torso at the end of these tube-looking arms. I could not see legs or feet, though. They appeared to float along the ground, as if by magic. When one of the Morelleons stopped moving, it seemed as if it was just another

21

peaceful plant, growing in the forest!

That's when I realized something. I quickly glanced around me, and sure enough, Previn and I had crept up beside a couple of these creatures, not even aware that they were here. "Duck!" I yelled before doing just that.

A claw just missed me as I tumbled away and rolled behind a tree. I heard Previn yell out in pain before a fiery flash went off, setting the Morelleon next to him on fire. With a scream, he started beating the creature with his mace, and burning chunks of it flew off in every direction. I darted out and used my magic dagger Magurk to slice off the cap of the one that had attacked me. I was surprised at how easy my blade cut through! The creature fell over without a sound. "Ha!" I yelled over to Previn. "My mother always taught me to beat my vegetables!"

At that moment, a concussive blast blew us into the air and we flew about twenty feet back into the forest. Lucky for us, we did not hit any trees. "What was that?!" I asked the cleric.

"A Sporelock!" Previn yelled back, "It's a spell casting Morelleon!"

We both hid behind a large tree and waited until another concussive blast shook the forest around us. "What do we do, now?" Previn asked me.

"Leave it to me," I said. "Just point out the Sporelock!"

Previn pointed his finger at the Morelleon with a bit more color on it. After the count of three, before the next blast, I ran from behind the tree holding Swatfly, my magic bow. I had struck the creature twice with my arrows before it could react. It wobbled for a few moments before hitting the ground with a large thud. Iris ran between my legs with a bark and headed over to Previn. I almost grinned, but I realized that he had barked, which meant he couldn't have brought the skeletal foot with him, or my Coin of Cheating!

I looked ahead and could see a skeletal toe sticking out from beneath the Sporelock, it had fallen on top of the foot. Iris must have panicked and ran before the creature hit the ground. All of a sudden, the forest was peaceful and quiet. That is, until I heard Onquay's voice yell out, "I think I heard something over here!"

The other Morelleons seemed to freeze in their places at the sound. I activated my Cloak of Blending and hid behind a tree. A grin slowly grew on my face as I realized that these two dragon droppings were about to be in for a big surprise. "Do you see him?" Apichat asked as he appeared from the woods, a few yards behind his counterpart.

"No," the white-eyed Onquay stated. "But I can feel a presence."

"It's times like these I'm glad you got bit by a vampire," Apichat stated. "It's heightened your senses."

It's too bad it didn't heighten his intelligence, I thought to myself. The large human lumbered around, snapping twigs and muttering; things he should have learned not to do while in the Crimson Roof Thieves Guild. It always amazed me how little these two had grown as rogues. In my opinion, they only graduated because the dean of my school just wanted to get rid of them! Onquay belched, then headed in my direction as if he could feel something. Then, he stated, "Look, I found something!"

I thought he had spotted me, but he walked right past me and pointed at a tree. "Look at this damage," he said to Apichat. "It's like something exploded."

Apichat began looking around the area and saw other trees just like it. "The source is from this direction," he said, walking to where the Morelleons were quietly standing in the dark.

I slowly moved around my tree, so I could watch the show. I couldn't wait to see the mushroom monsters spring to life and rip them to shreds. Hopefully, the bloodthirsty creatures would get full and move on, leaving my coin. "Look at the giant mushrooms," Onquay commented as they approached. "There's a weird looking one that fell over."

Just as they were about to get within the Morelleons reach, Iris barked. "What was that?" Apichat said, turning around. They could see Iris about fifteen yards away, come out from his hiding spot to bark more at them. "That dumb dog," I hissed under my breath. "He thinks they are after his bone!"

The two thugs turned from the Morelleons and walked over to the dog. "Hey," Onquay said. "This is Iris!"

"Onquay? Apichat?" Previn said, stepping out from his hiding spot. "I thought that was you two, but it's dark, so I couldn't see."

I couldn't believe it. The cleric knew the two imbeciles. "Good to see you and Iris," Apichat stated. "Oh, and Elfalfuh sends his regards. That last magical potion got rid of his migraine."

"His migraine probably left when you two did," I commented under my breath.

"You're welcome," Previn stated. "I'm just glad your boss makes such large donations to my temple clinic."

"Have you seen a weird-looking rogue pass through here?" Onquay asked as he rubbed Iris's belly. "A real simpleton. He has a weird green glowing eye."

"Oh, yes," Previn proclaimed. "He's another patient of mine. Is he a friend of yours?"

I put my face in my hand; I wanted to strangle the fool. "Why, yes," Apichat said. "We have a message for him from Elfalfuh. Just a few kind words."

"How nice!" the cleric said, happily. "He was just here, so he wouldn't have gone far."

"Oh, he can go far," Apichat stated. "He's pretty fast. The fool could be long gone."

"Phew," I thought to myself. Maybe now the idiots would go away.

"No, no," Previn said. "He was looking for a gold coin, you see?"

The two thugs looked at each other with a big grin. "You don't say?" they both said simultaneously.

I made a mental note to punch Previn after my next healing visit. I wanted to throw a rock at his head, but I didn't want to give away my location. Apichat and Onquay started looking around carefully. "You guys don't have to look around," Previn chirped. "He's probably just too scared to come out, like I was, because of the Morelleons."

"What are Morelleons?" Apichat asked.

Previn explained what had just happened and pointed at the creatures holding still over their fallen comrade. "We can take care of this," Onquay replied, pulling out his bow.

Less than a minute later, the two thugs had killed five of the six creatures while the other one moved away as quickly as it could move. "I hate vegetables," Onquay spat as they put their bows away.

"I guess you are jealous of higher life forms," I whispered under my breath, again.

Iris, not sensing any more danger, ran over and began barking at the fallen Sporelock. "What's he doing?" Onquay asked Previn.

"Oh, he just wants a bone that this Sporelock is lying on," Previn explained. "As a matter of fact, your friend's coin is stuck under there, as well."

"Coin?" Apichat repeated. "What coin?"

I could feel my blood pressure go up. "It's a special coin that he was willing to face any danger for, that's for sure," Previn chuckled. "What is it with you rogues and gold?"

Both Apichat and Onquay looked around, again, smiling broadly. "Well," Apichat began, "Let's get this special coin and make sure our 'friend' gets it back, tickety-boo!"

Onquay laughed and used his great strength to roll the body of the Sporelock over, revealing the skeletal foot and coin. "There it is," Previn declared happily. "Your friend should be ecstatic to know you have the coin!"

Onquay stood up, holding the coin in the air, while Iris ran below him and retrieved the skeletal foot. "Well, well, well," the oaf stated. "It looks like we have something special!"

He did not get to say anything further, because I did a full-frontal tackle on him, knocking the surprised man to the ground! With my cloak now deactivated, I rolled around behind Onquay, holding his back and placing Magurk to his throat. "Drop the coin!" I shouted.

Onquay knew better than to play games with me, so he did just that. "The coin is mine," Apichat stated, starting to walk forward.

"Take one more step, and he dies," I told the evil rogue.

"Go ahead," Apichat replied while taking another step. "Elfalfuh will just give me all the glory when I bring him this special coin of yours!"

25

Onquay braced for my slice, but Previn ran between us before anyone could react and grabbed the coin off the ground. "Stop, you guys!" he shouted. "Don't let some insignificant piece of money cause such a rift between friends!"

With that said, the cleric reached back his arm and hurled the coin high up into the woods. I dropped from Onquay's back and tried to follow the coin's direction with my eyes. First, we heard a tinging sound, like the coin had hit something, then a loud growl. We all stood there for a moment, wondering what to do. Then, out of nowhere, a black dragon ran out of the woods right toward us! We all dove out of the way as it snapped its teeth at us, trying to snag someone. Happily, it didn't get me; sadly, it missed Apichat and Onquay, as well.

The dragon appeared to be an elderly one, because of the gray forming on its black scales. It was still huge and did not look happy. I presumed it was asleep in the woods when the coin, which was stuck in a couple of scales by its eye, must have woken it up! As it passed, I instinctively grabbed its tail and held on for dear life. A few moments later, the dragon had taken flight, and we were gaining altitude. I could see Apichat and Onquay below shaking their fists at me, while Previn waved and Iris barked.

Chapter 6

I held on tight to the dragon's tail as we sailed high up in the night air. I was glad the ancient black dragon was so big, otherwise, I thought for sure he would notice me. To be on the safe side, I kept my blending cloak activated in case the dragon looked back. I didn't want him to see me, and then become a midnight snack for this beast. I'd rather plummet to my death than be any creature's bit of indigestion later.

From hundreds of feet up in the air, I could see the Unremembered Realms below. It was breathtaking. From the treetops to the distant city lights, I was reminded how large the realms really were. I wondered how I was going to get my coin from this decrepit old wyrm. Taking it on in battle was not going to be an option. Even at its advanced age, it was still one of the deadliest creatures in the realms. I thought about poisoning it, somehow, but even my most deadly are meant for monsters smaller than this one. The best it could do was give it a case of the hives, and then I could try to snag the coin whilst it was itching. I almost fell off when the dragon lurched a little to one side and began spiraling down toward the treetops below. I clutched the tail harder when the dragon did a swoop in the sky and banked in the direction of what I assumed to be Trippenfalls.

The water's crashing became louder and louder as we headed to an outcropping of rock right next to one of the many waterfalls which makes up the famous landmark. From my position, I could see another creature resting near the ledge, as if it was waiting for the dragon to arrive. It was a griffin. As we got closer, I could tell it was large and graying, as well. Its head perked up when the dragon landed. "How you doing tonight, Marv," the dragon asked.

"Oy," it began. "My back is killing me, Schleppe, nothing new."

"I thought you were seeing a cleric that you captured about that," Schleppe asked.

"I was," Marv stated. "But I ate him by mistake."

The dragon chuckled. "You old coot. You weren't wearing your glasses, again, were you?"

"I see just fine!" the griffin grunted. "I just didn't notice which villager I was grabbing in my nest. So, how is your night going?"

"Ugh," Schleppe began. "First, I ate an orc."

"You know they give you gas," Marv stated.

"I know, I know," the dragon replied. "But this one was chubby, so I caught him easy. Very tender and juicy."

The beast broke wind at that moment. I almost gagged out loud. My position at the tail was not helping me in the least. "Excuse me," the dragon said to the griffin.

"Then, my nap was interrupted by a bunch of noisy humans," Schleppe continued. "That's when I remembered it was our game night."

"It's a good thing," Marv said. "I would have been upset. I

barely got out of the nest. My sister-in-law came over, and my wife kept wanting to go over family sketches and kvetching about the neighbors. I swear I'm going to slaughter that group of valley giants. All they do stay up all night raising a ruckus!"

"I hear you," Schleppe complained. "The humans are growing in number in my area. I'd eat them all, but I'm afraid of putting on more weight. I've been watching my diet. I swear, just on my flight here, that I weighed more than usual."

"Don't get me started," Marv complained. "I ate a whole halfling village by myself once. I didn't save a single one. I felt terrible. Especially when my wife made me raid another one, I kept burping the whole time."

The black dragon chuckled and reached behind a boulder, pulling out a large sack. "You ready to roll some bones?" he asked before dumping out a bunch of skulls.

The griffon did the same thing with a sack of skulls he had hidden. Carefully, I dropped down from the tail and crept over to get a better look at what they were doing—scrawled on the ground was some kind of chart with numbers and symbols. The two creatures sat their gaming skulls off to either side of this bizarre gameboard and placed some fist-sized gems out for their wagers. I snuck up and was going to steal one, but the dragon grabbed it before I could. I froze, thinking that he could sense me, even though my cloak was still working.

"A little shmutz," Schleppe said, wiping off the gem before setting it back down in the center of the gaming area. "C'mon, Marv. Ante up."

The griffon did, with an emerald about the size of my head! These gems were big and beautiful! I started to daydream about cashing them in, then a skull flew past me, barely missing my face! "Out of bounds," Marv laughed. "You're such a shlemiel."

"Bah," Schleppe replied. "I'm just getting warmed up!"

This interaction pulled me out of my thoughts for a moment and helped me remember why I was there- to get back my magical Coin of Cheating! I could see it was still stuck between a couple of scales near the dragon's eye. I pondered how to approach the situation. During this time, the dragon and the griffon flicked skulls into the gaming area, letting out cheers or moans depending on where their skulls landed. Tiptoeing as best as I could, I approached near the dragon's face after he took his turn. I was hoping to do a quick grab-n-go. "Hold on!" the dragon yelled.

I felt my heart fall into my stomach. "That's a good roll!" Schleppe yelled.

"Oy," Marv started. "Look, the skull is half-cocked."

"That counts," the dragon replied. "I always let yours count!"

"I don't remember that," Marv shot back.

"You don't remember anything, you old bird!" Schleppe complained. "So how would you know?!"

While they argued, I took a moment to snatch a blue-colored gem and stuff it into one of my pockets. It wasn't the largest, but I could tell it would be high in value. "Ach!" the griffon gagged, his razor-sharp beak snapping.

"Not on the gameboard, please," Schleppe said, looking disgusted.

Marv turned from the gaming area and hacked up a hairball that was bigger than me! "Pardon me," he said. "Oh, look, a few more playing pieces!"

Using his claw, he reached into it and rolled out a few halfling skulls. "That's so disgusting," the dragon snorted, suppressing a laugh.

"You think when you hack up a ball of scales, it's any better?" Marv stated, flicking a halfling skull onto the board, knocking away one of Schleppe's.

"Touché," the dragon replied, eyeballing his next move.

I always wondered about how dragons kept themselves clean. It made me wonder if they had a rough tongue. If I wasn't careful, I'm sure I'd find out! "I keep smelling human," Marv stated before his move. "Are you sure you didn't eat any?"

"I keep smelling it, too," Schleppe said. "But I swear I missed them when I left. Hey, just between you and me, I could gnosh on a little human flesh right now."

"Me too!" Marv laughed. "I wish we could get some delivery."

Being a little nervous, I started backstepping. I didn't see the halfling skull behind me, and I stumbled and fell onto the ground. When that happened, my Cloak of Blending was deactivated. I was lying on the ground in front of the two.

"Wow!" Schleppe stated. "That was quick!"

"We didn't even place an order, yet," Marv stated. "Maybe I should make another wish!"

"I get the head," Schleppe said, sniffing me.

"I always get stuck with the bottom half," Marv complained. "This time, I get the head!"

"Why don't you two geezers flip a coin for it?" I asked, trying to stall.

They both looked at me for a moment, then blinked. "I don't have a coin," Marv stated. "Do you have one, Schleppe? All I brought were my gems."

The dragon shook his head. "All my gold is back at my lair," he answered. "I don't usually carry loose change."

Luckily, Marv's eyes weren't that good, and he hadn't spotted the small coin lodged above his friend's left eye. "I can pull one from your ear, dragon," I said to Schleppe. "Maybe, if you are impressed with my magic, you'll let me go."

"I can't make any promises," the dragon stated. "But I can try to make your death quick."

"That seems fair," Marv said. "I'd take that deal!"

I sighed for a moment and hung my head. That's when I remembered the skull on the space by my feet that Schleppe controlled, and that gave me an idea! "I'll take that deal," I said reluctantly. "Now, check your ear, dragon."

The dragon smiled and checked both ears. "There's nothing in either ear," he declared.

"And nothing in between," Marv added, laughing.

"Quit being a yutz," Schleppe retorted. "Just show me the trick, rogue."

"Sure thing," I said, jumping up.

While they watched me get to my feet, they failed to notice that I nudged the halfling skull over a line onto the next space. I walked over to the dragon, who lowered his head. "Punim de

30

tuches!" I shouted before using my minor telekinesis power to pull the coin from the scales into my hand while reaching by the dragon's ear.

Then, I turned around with the coin in the air and walked back out between them. "I'll bet you've never seen that before!" I cried out.

Marv yawned. "Can you just flip the coin so we can eat you, now?"

Schleppe didn't look impressed, either. But that was okay; I figured these two would eat me even if they were impressed. "Alright, alright," I said. "I had to give it a try. So, griffon, what are you calling, heads or tails?"

"I'll stick with heads," he said, licking his beak. "Now flip it, flip it good."

I looked over at Schleppe and he nodded in agreement. I know I had the magical Coin of Cheating in my hand, but even it couldn't help me in this situation. So, I had to rely on my trickery to get out of this mess. We all watched as the coin flipped up in the air. It seemed to fall in slow motion before finding its place on the ground between us all. "Heads!" Marv shouted. "It's heads! Today is my lucky day!"

"Ugh," Schleppe grumped. "Such luck. Go ahead, bite his head off, and toss me the rest!"

Before he could grab me, I held up my hand and shouted, "Whoa! Wait a minute! Wasn't this skull over on your space a little while ago, dragon?"

The black dragon looked on at the skull and frowned at the griffon. "Well, well, well," he said unhappily. "Maybe it isn't luck after all. You've been cheating again, Marv!"

"I swear I didn't move it! I don't know what happened!" he yelled. "You must have moved it, Schleppe. In case you lost the coin toss!"

The dragon rolled his eyes. "You're just trying to use false allegations to justify your usual treachory!"

"Here we go, again," Marv yelled back. "You know I haven't cheated at our game in years."

31

"Wait a minute," Schleppe paused. "You don't think…"

"Rogue!" they both shouted simultaneously.

I would have shouted "Jinx!" but I was too busy running toward the edge of the outcropping. My Boots of Speeding helped tremendously at moments like this.

"Get back here," was all I heard before diving off the edge by the waterfall.

I could feel the air whip around me, but I couldn't hear the two elderly beasts anymore over the roar of the waterfall. This action was not the first time I had jumped into this waterfall, but it was the first time I'd done it at night. I hoped I wasn't anywhere near the rocky outcroppings that protruded just above the surface. I braced for a watery impact, hoping the spot I landed would be deep enough for me to live. I did have a smile on, though. It felt good, knowing my coin was back in my hand, at last!

Chapter 7

After landing in the river below, I was surprised at how refreshing the water was. I was also happy that my head wasn't split open from any rocks! The stream flowing eastward was called the Unnamed River. It was titled that way because nobody could agree on a name for it. It had a reputation as being quite deadly, too. Besides drowning, there were flesh-eating fish, a strong undertow, and a legendary creature known as the Loch Mess. They called the monster that, because that was all that would be left of you, if you had the misfortune of making her acquantaince. Messy, as some call her, stayed mostly in Lake Netherbottom, but rumor had it that she made her way up the Unnamed River, once in a while.

I wasn't worried about the other dangers at that moment. I was quite happy that I landed here. It felt good after spending time roaming around the sewers of Neverspring. I couldn't stay in the water long, though; I was in my full gear and it was making it difficult to swim.

When I broke the surface, I was fully expecting Schleppe or

Marv to be in the sky, circling me from above. To my surprise, they weren't. Maybe they didn't think it was worth the bother. It didn't matter to me; I had my coin, and all I had to do was swim to shore and make my way back to the Palm Eye Finger Magic Shop. Even though I had hidden the key to the place in a secret location, I was worried that Schmendrake might come across it. Perhaps he would disable all the traps that Bub and Lar had set up. As I swam, I could feel the powerful current beneath me, which made me more than a little nervous.

I didn't like being in the river at night, because the water was dark, making it hard to see if anything was coming at you from below, which was always a strong possibility in the Unremembered Realms. I was swiftly being pulled eastward along the Unnamed River toward Netherbottom Lake, which connects all four realms.

I was only a few yards from the shore when I felt something brush past my feet. Before I could paddle harder, something grabbed my legs and pulled me under the water. I grabbed for my magic dagger, Magurk, but it was too late. I felt something poke at me, and a surge of power shot through my body, making everything go black.

When I gained consciousness, I saw that I had been strapped to an upright wooden table. I was still wet, and all my gear was lying on a bench in front of me. It appeared that I was inside a cave that had been turned into a laboratory. There were all sorts of vials with colored liquids, powders in containers, and books. My opened journal sat on the table next to my pack with my magical Coin of Cheating resting between its pages. I tried to use my minor telekinesis power to grab it, but it was too far away. It didn't help that my wrists were tied tightly to the table!

The room wasn't lit by torches, just by little orbs that floated about six inches from the ceiling. There were multiple bookshelves along the walls and a wooden door that must've led out to somewhere. I could also see two tables across the room that were just like mine; only they were back-to-back. On one, was a dead human male that looked like he had been rotting for a while. His mouth was open like he had died mid-scream. On the table behind him was a lizardman, who was also dead. There were claw marks all over the table, as if it had tried to frantically escape before whatever killed it finished the job.

The weirdest part was that both wore strange-looking half helmets on their heads with tubes coming out of them. The tubes connected one to another and an odd-looking device sitting on a table next to them. Around the device were mostly empty vials that looked as if they had been poured into a hole in the top of the contraption. "What a horrible way to die," I mumbled, not feeling good about my situation.

"Gwai Lo?" I heard a voice say from behind me. "Is that you?"

"Froghat?" I replied, recognizing the voice.

"I can't believe it!" the wizard shouted excitedly. "What are the odds of us both being captured!?"

"Lucky me," I sighed, hanging my head.

Just when I thought things couldn't get any worse, it turned out that I was about to meet my maker with one of the people of the realms that annoyed me the most! I have adventured with the old wizard more than I'd like to admit, and it seemed like fate always brought us together. I swear, if I ever found the fool who was writing my life story, I'd punch him in the mouth!

"Ozone is here, too," the wizard happily stated. "He's in a small cage on a table to my right."

I looked over to my left and noticed the frog familiar just sitting there, staring at us. I pulled at my bonds for a moment, testing them. "What is this place?" I asked.

"It looks like an unlicensed alchemist's lab," Froghat answered. "There're magic components laying around here that I've never seen before."

The wizard started yammering on and on about what he thought the components might be, so I cut him off before dying of boredom. "I hate to ask," I sighed. "But how did you end up here?"

"Oh, I couldn't sleep at the party's camp," the wizard explained. "Stretch Markus was snoring loudly, as usual, so I thought I'd take Ozone out for a stroll. Besides, Pickenfling the halfling must have eaten something bad, because..."

"Yada, yada," I interrupted, wanting to cut off any gross stories about the halfling cleric. "Just cut to the chase, okay?"

"Oh," Froghat said. "Anyway, I was stopping by the edge of the water, getting some frothy river scum for Ozone, when a weird looking creature rose from the water and struck me with a staff!"

"Those would be my shock troopers," a gruff voice broke in loudly. "I'm glad to see the both of you have woken up. You've been unconscious most of the day."

When I looked up, I could see a lizardman dressed in some robes and carrying a leather side bag. On either side of him were two halfling sized turtoids that stood upright and held staves that glowed blue on the ends. They were ugly and looked eager to cause us some pain. "These shrimps wouldn't have got me if I hadn't just finished bravely fighting off a dragon and griffon, single-handedly," I stated menacingly. "And once I'm free from here, I'm going to eat some turtoid soup, I'm starving!"

"It looks like Test Subject B woke up on the wrong side of the table," the lizardman hissed, or chuckled; it was hard to tell.

"Wait a minute," I said, realizing something awful. "You mean to tell me this frog brain behind me is Test Subject A, and I'm just a B?!"

"A is for awesome!" Froghat stated cheerfully.

This insult only made me madder. Then, the lizardman stepped closer, removed some vials from his side bag, and placed them on the table. "Why wouldn't I list him as A? He's more of a threat! He is a powerful mage! You? You're just another run-of-the-mill rogue."

"He's never run a mill in his life!" Froghat chimed in from behind me, "or have you, Gwai Lo?"

"Wait a minute," the lizardman said, stepping even closer. "I've heard of you. You're the Ghost Man!"

"Thanks, Froghat," I said. "Thanks a lot!"

"Word from my old village is that you killed a lot of my old associates who belonged to the Doom Cough Cult!"

"It was a misunderstanding," I started to explain. "You see, a lot of your friends are idiots. They didn't understand that I would kill them if they didn't let me go. Starting to get the picture, halfling breath?"

"Good one," Froghat laughed, "That's funny, because lizardmen like eating halflings!"

The lizardman rolled his eyes almost at the same time as I did. "I noticed you have the left hand of a lizardman," the alchemist stated, looking down at my hand. "How did that happen?"

"Let's just say that when I needed help, one of your own decided to give me a hand," I sneered.

"Maybe I was wrong about you two," he hissed before ordering his shelled soldiers to tighten our bonds and place the half-helmets securely on our heads. "By the way," the lizardman stated without turning around, "My name is Thinktinkeron, and I'm the realm's greatest alchemist. I want you always to remember that, because I'm going to change your life!"

The whole time we talked, I tried using my telekinesis to slowly pick the lock that held my leather wrist straps into place. I tried to be as secretive as I could. One wrong move would mean a shock from one of the turtoids. While I was concentrating, Froghat asked the alchemist a hundred questions. "How are you mixing those potions? What do they taste like? And what time could we eat?"

Thinktinkeron suddenly walked between us and poured whatever mixture he made into a bubbling jar that was similar to the one on other table that I saw. "You ready, boys?" he laughed.

I finally got the lock picked and quickly undid the other wrist, but then I felt it, a surge of energy blast through my body that shook me like a lightning bolt! I began to see swirling colors all around me, stars, yellow flashes, my mother's face sticking out her tongue at me, and then dancing frogs all around me and strumming their tongues like they were playing lutes!

Then, everything went black. When I started to come around, I heard the voice of Thinktinkeron shouting, "It worked! It finally worked!"

That's also when I noticed I had been moved. I blinked a few times to clear my eyes and could see I had moved to where Froghat

36

was strapped down. It must have been some chemically induced teleport! At least, that's what I thought for a moment, until I heard my voice speak out from behind me, "This is so cool!"

Horror crept over me as I looked down at my hands. They were older and both human! I looked over to my right, and Ozone croaked at me. My head felt cold, like I didn't have hair. "Aigh!" I yelled. "What have you done!"

"He switched our bodies!" Froghat, I mean Froghat from my body, yelled. "This is so awesome!"

Thinktinkeron laughed. "I thought the success of my experiment would change your minds!"

The lizardman was excited and gave his short shock troopers some low-fives. I decided to give my telekinesis powers a try. It was to no avail; even my secret power was now in the hands of the bumbling wizard! I pulled at the straps, but it was no use; they were as tight as ever. "Struggle all you want, ghost man," Thinktinkeron stated, walking over to face me. "But this is only the beginning of the experiments! I'm going to take this to new levels and change the realms! First you and the wizard, then I'll be switching minds with the King of Cloverose!"

The lizardman started into a loud cackle, but suddenly let out a loud "Gurk!" before falling to the floor in front of me! My dagger, Magurk, was sticking out of his back! Froghat stood before me, smiling. "Your body is so agile and quiet," he remarked, doing a little dance. "I can be fast and quiet; no one even sees me coming!"

"Quit dancing around like that," I warned him. "You make me look foolish."

Froghat regained his composure and walked over to the cage with Ozone the frog in it. "How did you get my bonds loose before we switched bodies?" he asked.

"Um…never mind that. Where are the guards?" I asked.

"They were the first to go," Froghat laughed. "I'm so stealthy!"

"Would you please get me out of here!?" I demanded. "Why'd you free the frog first?! Wait, don't put him on top of my head!"

I watched in horror as he removed my cowl and placed his slimy amphibian familiar on top of my body's head with a goofy-looking grin. I made a mental note to myself never to smile anymore, because it appeared utterly absurd. "This is so unfair," I told him as I struggled against my bonds. "I can't even cast any of your spells!"

Froghat searched the body of Thinktinkeron and found the key to my bonds. I felt completely useless as I watched my body fumble with the key trying to unlock me. I had been picking locks since I was a small child, and here I was, waiting for a lint brain like Froghat to rescue me! Finally, the lock popped, and I grabbed the key and undid my other wrist. I rubbed my newly bald head before marching over to a table to look at some of the books. Among them, were alchemy periodicals, a halfling recipe book, and finally, his notebook.

"What are you doing?" asked the wizard.

"I'm looking at how to reverse this," I mumbled, scanning over the pages. "Thinktinkeron had to have been keeping notes."

I quickly realized that it was no use. All the writing was written in wizardry jargon. "Can you read this?" I said, shoving an open book into Froghat's hands.

"Of course not," he claimed. "I'm a rogue!"

After that, he burst out into some laughter that he, for some reason, thought I would laugh along with. He stopped after realizing I was giving him an icy stare. "Ahem," he coughed while putting his eyes to the book. "Uh-huh, mmm, yes, I see."

"What is it? What does it say?" I asked.

"I don't know," he shrugged. "It looks like a bunch of gibberish with upside-down numbers."

Ozone did a small croak. "Oh," the wizard replied before turning the book right side up. "Thanks, Ozone."

I buried my face in my hands and grumbled. I couldn't believe my future laid in the hands of this nitwit. Not only that, but if he failed in finding a solution, I would be reminded of it every time I looked into a mirror! "Just read the book," I sighed.

As the wizard poured over the text, I noticed that my stomach was growling. By the time the wizard screamed, "Aha!" I had already made some turtoid soup.

38

We ate while he told me what he had learned. "Well, the good news is that this will eventually wear off," he began. "The bad news is that we don't know how long it will last."

"What are we talking about, here? Days, weeks, or even years?" I asked, feeling flustered. "I mean, I can't go see Amberfawn like this; I'm old and reek of moldy lily pads!"

Then, it dawned on me. If others found out that Froghat and I switched bodies, I'd be the laughingstock of the Crimson Roof Thieves Guild! I'd probably be the butt of many frog jokes, and they'd likely serve me flies at the next alumni luncheon.

"We have to pretend to be one another," I said, wiping my travel spoon down and placing it back into Froghat's, I mean, my gear pack. "This has to be our little secret."

"Are you joking?" Froghat asked. "I hope so, cuz I can't wait to tell the others back at camp! I'll be their new hero!"

My blood was starting to boil, but I took a deep breath and relaxed. "Listen," I said, "If you keep quiet and play along, I'll make you an official honorary Crimson Roof Guild Member. I'll even get you a secret pendant, then show you our even secreter handshake."

Froghat was beaming, by that point. "It's a deal!" he said, grinning from ear-to-ear.

Of course, I had made everything up, but the goof wouldn't know any better. I'd buy some trinket at the next Flip-N-Wink and tell him not to show it to anybody.

"Hopefully, this wears off in a short period, and things can get back...to...normal..." I slowly said as I saw my face with soup smeared all over it.

Froghat was a notoriously messy eater, while I hated to spill a drop. "Please wipe your face," I told him. "I don't eat like that; that's a dead giveaway that something's wrong."

"Well, then you've got to make a mess with your face," Froghat said, crossing his arms. "I'm not the only one who's got to convince others, here."

I nodded and picked up one of the turtoids' magical shock sticks. To my surprise, it grew in length to fit my size. "I love magic," Froghat said, observing the strange weapon. "Can I have it when we're back to normal?"

"Of course," I explained, "But if I see one nick on Magurk, I'm going to have you strangle myself!"

"You won't change your mind?" he pressed.

"I already have!" I hissed. "And so have you!"

Froghat and I got our wits together and did a quick search of the lab, then the guards' quarters, and then of Thinktinkeron, himself. He had a large sack of gold and many components for spells that Froghat was going gaga over. I didn't care much about those, but he kept stuffing all my pockets.

Most importantly, though, I made sure my Coin of Cheating was tucked away into a pocket of the robe I was now wearing. I wasn't about to let a halfwit like Froghat carry it, even if he was in current possession of my body! After a few minutes of exploring, we found an exit that led back out into the realms. The stars were just starting to show as the sun set. "What a waste of a day," I grumbled as we began to search for a good place to cross the water.

To our delight, a few dozen yards from the door, hidden partially by a bush, was a small rowboat that we could use to cross the Unnamed River. We loaded the gold and other supplies we took into it and pushed it out into the water. By the time I started rowing, the moon had replaced the sun completely.

Chapter 8

The boat rocked back and forth a little as I paddled it across the river. The moon was bright, so it made it easy to see the upcoming forest in front of us. I missed my lich eye, which helped me see even better at night. It drove me crazy that Froghat was using it right now, and I depended on his observation skills. "Just remember to keep your eyes open," I reminded him. "I have somewhere to be, and until we're changed back, you'll have to come with…"

That's when we hit a stony outcropping in the river. The boat lurched but did not turn over. "You're supposed to be watching where we are going!" I hissed at the wizard. "That's why I let you be in the front of the boat!"

"Sorry," Froghat replied. "I was just daydreaming a bit. You know, about being an honorary rogue."

"You don't daydream at night," I said, flustered. "That only happens during the day; you regularly dream at night. You're supposed to be watching where we're going, because you have the better vision, now!"

"But I'm not asleep," Froghat explained. "How can it be a night dream when I'm not sleeping? You know what? I should write a poem about daydreaming at night! I could sell it to a bard and make a ton of gold! Where's my quill?"

After stating that, he turned around toward me, searching himself. "Keep your eye on the water!" I yelled, but it was too late.

The rowboat hit another outcropping, and a hole broke into its side. Water came pouring in, and soon we were both swimming the rest of the way to shore. Luckily, the water was now turtoid-free. Swimming wasn't easy because of the current, but we managed. Both of us laid on the dry land for a moment and caught our breath. "I think you have my quill," Froghat said to me between pants of breath.

I seriously wanted to strangle him, at that point, but I didn't want to damage my own body. Besides, I didn't want to be stuck in this one forever. The frog slime drying on my head made it itchy.

"Remind me to clobber you later," I said, panting heavily. "We could have been drowned, you old fool!"

"No way," he laughed. "This body of yours never seems to get tired! I wouldn't have gotten tired at all if I hadn't had to carry that large sack of gold!"

"The gold!" I shouted, sitting up quickly. "Where is the gold?!"

"Well," Froghat mumbled. "I kind of had to let it go…"

"What?!" I yelled, jumping to my feet. "I can't believe that even you could do something that idiotic!"

"It weighed too much," he shrugged. "What was I supposed to do? Drown with it?"

"I would have!" I growled, shaking my fist at him. "Now go

back in there and…"

It was no use; I ran my hand over my face as he stood there looking at me, dumbly, green eye blinking. "Ugh," I finally muttered. "Let's just go to the camp; I need a warm fire to dry off!"

"That, I can do!" Froghat smiled before standing up and marching into the trees. "Oh, and here is Ozone. The rest of the party may get suspicious if he's on my head."

The forest was dark and a little chilly. I couldn't wait to get to the campfire and feel its heat on my hands. I could see Froghat swatting at mosquitoes as he walked in front of me. I could hear their buzzing, too, but Ozone's tongue shot out and gobbled them up if they got anywhere close. For once, I didn't mind having the slimy pest on my head.

My feet stayed wet as the dry ground gave way to some spongey, moist moss. We had entered a swampy section of the forest. "Where is the camp?" I asked. "Why in the realms are you camping out in a swamp?"

"We're on a rescue mission," Froghat answered while stepping over a wet, rotting log. "Pickenfling's cousin, Skole, was captured by some lizardmen. We wanted to catch them before they sliced him up for a meal. You know how much lizardmen crave halfling flesh."

I nodded in acknowledgment. I, personally, found halflings to be total weirdos, but lizardmen seemed to find them quite succulent. I hated fighting lizardmen, because their hide was tough to pierce. Yet, because of that, they were highly sought after for making ladies' handbags. It made for a great taunt I could always use on them. "Do you prefer to be skinned for a dainty carry all, or would you rather be an over the shoulder bag?" I'd ask, just to enrage them.

Not all lizardmen are savages, though; I'd been a guildmate of one who was civil. His breath reeked of pickled, halfling feet, and he loved to eat rodents raw. I'd laugh at him every time he hurt himself, setting mouse traps, or as he called them, snack trays. Suddenly, my thoughts were interrupted when I felt Ozone lick the top of my head.

42

"This thing won't go to the bathroom on me, will it?" I asked.

The wizard just smirked at me; his glowing green eye seemed to brighten.

"Oh, you'll find out!" he laughed.

I mumbled to myself about eating frog legs for dinner, and I felt the amphibian shift around on my head. Its little suction cup toes held it firmly in place on my bald scalp. It was a weird feeling, and I couldn't wait to get it off me. "Oh, look," Froghat whispered, "he fell asleep, still licking your head! Aw, I never can get over how cute he is!"

I ignored the wizard and kept walking, trying to disregard the sticky sensation of the annoying creature's tongue stuck to my head. Instead, I focused on the trees, bushes, and plant life. I didn't want to run into any surprises, like poison ivy or sharpened stick traps! The moonlight cast many shadows, and in the Unremembered Realms, that meant danger. I, myself, have killed many enemies by hiding in shadows; it's like an invisibility spell, but cheaper.

I spotted the small glow of fire about the same time that Froghat whispered, "There's the camp."

I was still cold, and I couldn't wait to sit in front of the fire and warm up. "Remember," I told the wizard, "I'm you, and you're me."

"No problem," he replied while picking up his pace. "This should be fun."

I sighed, knowing that it wouldn't be, and followed after him.

"Gwai Lo!" Stretch Markus shouted happily, standing up from the log he was sitting on. "What are you doing here?"

At first, Froghat hat didn't respond, then he remembered. "Oh! Yeah, that's me!"

I did a facepalm. Suddenly, Pickenfling, the halfling cleric, was there, hugging Froghat's leg. I would have kicked him, but Froghat just laughed. "You are well-liked," the wizard stated, looking back at me.

"Ixnay on the ricktay," I hissed.

That's when I noticed Dogchauw, the half gnoll fighter, curled

43

up by the fire, still asleep. "Some watchdog," I mumbled, walking up next to him and sitting down on the log.

The fire felt great. It's warmth swept over the front of me. I felt the blood rush back to my fingers as I wiggled them closer to the flame. "Isn't it great to see Gwai Lo again, gang?" I stated. "He bravely rescued me, once again, even though I lost all his gold. I think we should all take up a collection."

They ignored what I said, and instead hung on Froghat's every word. "It sure would be nice to rest in your magically enhanced Hammock of Snoozing," the wizard said to Stretch Markus.

"Consider it done," the overweight ranger stated. "I'll even fluff Froghat's pillow for you. You don't mind giving up your pillow, do you, Froghat?"

Frowning, I reluctantly agreed. I didn't want to, and the thought of sleeping on the ground with a rock for a headrest made me angry. I thought it might be nice to put the pillow over the goofy's wizard's face, but he was in my body, and I didn't want to kill myself.

"Don't worry, Froghat," Pickenfling stated cheerfully, "You can use mine! You know, we were worried about you after you disappeared last night! We're glad you made it back!"

The halfling ran into his tent and came out with a heavily stained pillow. Before I could say no, Froghat looked at me and nodded. He knew I was going to say no, or at least throw it in the fire! He held his finger up to his lips, then pulled it down quickly when Pickenfling looked back at him. "Fine," I stated, with a forced grin. "Ozone and I appreciate it."

The smell of the pillow was quite intense, so with a finger and thumb, I cautiously laid it down next to me. "So, guys," I began as they finally gathered around the fire. "What's the plan for rescuing Snole?"

"Skole," everyone stated, at the same time, correcting me.

"Skole, yeah, whatever," I said. "What's the plan."

"You said you were going to come up with a plan when you went out, Froghat," Pickenfling stated. "But since Gwai Lo is here, I think he should do it."

44

"I agree," Stretch Markus cut in. "Most of your plans are terrible, wizard. No offense."

"None taken," I reluctantly replied.

I agreed, but as of that moment, I knew the direction of where this conversation was going, and I didn't like it, especially when I saw the large grin on my own face across from me. "First off," Froghat started. "I think all of my, er, I mean, Froghat's plans are well thought out and near-genius. But, for this instance, I will gladly share my battle plan to face off against the lizardmen!"

Stretch Markus and Pickenfling nodded in agreement, but Dogchauw just groaned and rolled over, letting out a slight "woof" like he was dreaming about chasing a wagon or something. "Well," I said, crossing my arms. "What's the plan?"

Froghat leaned closer to the fire to add a dramatic effect. "I say we, um....face them head-on, yelling a scary battle cry as we enter their camp!"

"Brilliant!" Pickenfling shouted, jumping to his feet while clapping. "Just brilliant!"

Stretch turned to me and nodded, "I can't argue with that logic!"

"Are you kidding me?!" I said, standing up. "You'll lose any attempt at surprise!"

Froghat shook his cowled head. "I don't think so, Gwa...Froghat," he stated confidently. "You see, that is the surprise! They will never expect to be hit head-on in open sunlight!"

I buried my head in my hands. I wished the experiment, trapping us in one another's body, would wear off; this whole situation was going to get me killed! I couldn't even run away, because the nitwit controlling my body would get himself slaughtered, and I'd be trapped with a frog licking my head forever!

"I need to lie down," I groaned to myself.

"Sure thing, Froghat," Froghat said while giving me a thumbs up.

"Hey, who's got first watch?" I asked.

"Dogchauw, of course," Pickenfling said, "You know that."

"This mutt couldn't stay awake in a thunderstorm," I began. "I uh, oh, I mean. 'Chauw is doing great."

I raised my eyebrows and stared at Froghat, who jumped in.

"This um, biscuit brain has passed out," he stumbled, never taking his eyes off me. "Therefore, I, the trusty rogue, shall do the honors."

The wizard gave a small shrug, but the others didn't seem to notice. "Once again, Gwai Lo is right," Stretch said, "I nominate him to do it. This swamp is a dangerous area, and he never falls asleep."

"Yes," Froghat said triumphantly. "I'll do it!"

"But you always nod off first!" I said before catching myself. "I mean, thank the realms, Gwai Lo. Because I always tend to nod off, leaving the party in incredible danger, like a complete nincompoop!"

"You can all count on me," Froghat stated proudly before letting out a big yawn.

The wizard's left eye started to droop, "Nobody gets by me!"

After everyone fell asleep, I watched Froghat circle the camp a few times before leaning on a tree and dozing out! I watched in silence as a squirrel climbed across a small branch and broke it before it fell on top of the wizard. He didn't even stir! What took the cake was a large snake slithered around his legs before I ran over and shooed it away. I had to wake him up and take his place before he got us all killed!

"Hunh...what..." he mumbled and stumbled his way to the comfy hammock Stretch had set up for him.

My turn at the guard was uneventful, and I eventually got my turn to sleep after waking up Pickenfling to take over. I'm always hard on the gross little halfling, but I give credit where it due. He never falls asleep on the job, and he knows his healing magic. It's just horrible when you have to let him touch you to cast said spells. It was for moments like that you would wish you had a disinfectant cantrip to cast. I swear, it's the only time I ever want to be a mage.

"Froghat, wake up," someone said as I blinked my eyes open. "We don't want to miss out on Gwai Lo's awesome rescue plan!"

"Ugh," I rolled over, but only to see Ozone the Frog staring directly into my eyes.

I rolled back over to see Stretch Markus looking down at me. He had donut crumbs around his unshaved, smiling mouth. To this day, I never understood how he always had donuts. We could be traveling across the Barrendry Desert for a week, and the overweight ranger would somehow pull out a cruller or bugbear claw.

For breakfast, we had roasted snake and squirrel; apparently, Dogchauw had caught them when he finally woke up. The half gnoll could sniff out anything if it were wandering close enough for him to catch a scent. "I don't know how Dogchauw finds all this food," Froghat said, chewing with his mouth open. "I wonder how he tracked these down!"

"I wonder," I remarked before he gave me a thumbs up.

After quickly packing up our gear, we followed the trail that Stretch Markus had found and stayed on it for half an hour. That's when we heard the familiar hissing chuckle of a lizardman. Taking cover behind some vine-like bushes, we could see a tall lizardman rubbing spices all over a halfling, who was tied to a tree, wearing only his undergarments. The halfling spat at the creature, which only made it laugh harder.

"Skole!" Pickenfling shouted.

We all ducked as the lizardman glanced our way. Luckily, he dismissed the noise and continued with his breakfast preparation. The monster was talking to Skole, but I couldn't hear a word. Froghat's body's old ears were not helpful in situations like these. "What's he saying, Gwai Lo?"

Froghat looked intently at the two while the rest of us patiently waited. "Umm…something about a failed rescue attempt… oh, and how dumb…could…they be…to…"

"Attack head-on in the morning," came a voice from behind us, finishing his sentence.

We all slowly turned around.

Three muscular lizardmen were standing there, pointing their razor-sharp spears at us. "I thought I heard something," Froghat stated, raising his hands.

"Why in the realms didn't you say anything?!" I said through clenched teeth.

"I didn't want to ruin your plan," the wizard sputtered.

"It wasn't my plan, you dolt! It was yours! You're me!" I yelled.

"Oh, yeah," he laughed. "My bad!"

"What are you two talking about?" Pickenfling asked, looking perplexed. "Is there something going on here that we need to know about?!"

"Look," said one of the lizardman, "Our lunch is all confused. How cute. Capture the halfling and kill the rest of these clowns!"

With that said, one of the creatures thrust his spear at Stretch Markus, who instinctively turned around, trying to avoid the blow. The tip of the spear went into his pack, and when it pulled back out, six frosted chocolate donuts tumbled out onto the ground. The lizardmen were not expecting that, and they paused for a moment. That's when Stretch glanced behind him and saw his confections in the mushy moss and leaves. "My donuts!" he yelled in a fit of rage.

The lizardman who stabbed at him could not react fast enough; the overweight ranger was on top of him faster than a stripe on a frosted éclair! The rest of us wasted no time and pulled out our weapons, just as the remaining two lizardmen pounced. I ducked a few spear thrusts and rolled out of the way of a claw swipe. Dogchauw swung wildly at another one with his sword while Pickenfling bit its ankle, causing it to cry out in pain.

Froghat just danced around the one I was fighting, doing weird poses like he was a ninja or something. "I'm a rogue, not a ninja, pea-brain!" I yelled at him while barely getting sliced on the arm from the spear's deadly sharp tip.

By this time, the wizard had circled to the back of the lizard-man. "Oh. Okay," Froghat shouted back. "Quickly, reach into my left pocket and throw out the twig and spider tongue; I'll say the words!"

Not wanting to get stabbed, I reached into the pocket and threw whatever was in it at the creature. With a few mumbled words and a flash of purple light, the lizardman screamed out in pain, and within seconds, he morphed into a Chamelion, a deadly creature that resembled a lion and a chameleon. It had claws and sharp-looking teeth, but it could also blend into its surroundings and be nearly invisible! "Oops," Froghat yelled out. "I forgot that you're on the opposite side. I meant your right pocket!"

I dove out of the way just as the creature lunged at me, and it sailed straight over. I could feel Ozone clinging harder to my bald head as I reached into my right pocket and threw the contents in the direction of the creature. Finally, as Froghat mumbled some words, a fiery explosion blew up in front of the monster, sending it fifteen feet in the air! It landed on the ground with a thump before it rolled around, trying to put the fire out.

I couldn't believe the wizard had gotten something right! With a whimpering howl, the Chamelion ran off into the swamp. When I turned around to give the wizard a thumbs up, I noticed that he was now making his way over to the lizardman, who was slowly retreating from Dogchauw's attacks. Pickenfling was lying on the ground, unconscious. Stretch had punched his lizardman to death and was now up and coming to help. I jumped over the halfling as I, too, made my way to help out. I couldn't see the other lizardman who had been with the captured halfling, but I assumed he ran off. When we were almost close enough to fight the remaining monster, I heard a chop and a snap, like a rope had just been cut.

Before I could feel the embarrassment of not detecting this trap, I felt myself being pulled upward in the air, inside a net! I was crushed with my face mushed up against Markus's big belly. "I can barely breathe!" I mumbled into his vast belly button. "This is so gross!"

I heard the lizardmen laugh as they walked around us. "This should be fun," one hissed. "Look at these losers."

"What's this?" the other said, limping over and kneeling below where I was hanging. "A gold coin, with weird symbols on it!"

My Coin of Cheating! My blood boiled as I watched the bloodied creature hold it up for me to see. It must have fallen out of my pocket when the net pulled us up. I struggled a bit, but it was no use; it only pushed me harder into Markus's flab. "Say goodnight, ladies," laughed one of the lizardmen as he pulled out a small bag of sleeping dust.

Before I could wriggle around anymore, things went black. I'm not sure how much time had passed, but when I awoke, I could feel that I'd been tied to a tree. My party was, too, except for Pickenfling, who was tied on a spit with an apple in his mouth. They had stripped him down to his undergarments, whose cleanliness I won't describe, in case anybody reading this is having a meal. One of the lizardmen was trying to start a fire using the kindling below the foul little halfling.

"Stop wetting yourself over the wood, you little creep," I heard the lizardman muttering.

Pickenfling gave me a wink when he realized I had just woken up. "He can go all day," Skole laughed from the tree he was tied to, trying to taunt the green scaly creature. "He has bladder issues."

"It's true," Dogchauw stated as he had woken up. "Pickenfling wets more trees than I do!"

While the two lizardmen argued over how to start the fire properly, I was slowly trying to undo the rope that held me to the tree. I may not have had my telekinesis, at the moment, but I was still a master of escape. I have to admit, though, the arthritis in Froghat's old hands was slowing me up a bit. I just had to stall the two for a while. Before I could come up with a plan, Froghat decided to join the conversation. "You two don't scare me," he began. "If you didn't notice, I have a lizardman's hand. I sliced it off one of your cousins, just for a laugh. Now I'm looking for a new head!"

I just shook my head at the lame attempt. "That was a lousy taunt," one of them said while the other one nodded in agreement. "Are you sure you weren't dropped on your noggin as a child?"

"Do you want us to kill you now or wait till later," the wizard said through gritted teeth as the two approached him. "You can kill me, but my spirit will live on!"

"No, it won't, you dolt!" I shouted at him angrily. After all, he was still in my body!

"Let's torture the rogue," one said to the other. "We'll see how tough he is after a few cracks of this barbed whip!"

I hadn't even noticed the long leathery whip that one had carried with him. "Not the face! Not the face!" I cried out.

With a gasp, I watched as Froghat moved his head as a lizardman tried to punch him and hit the tree instead. "Owww!" it cried out. "I think I broke my claw!"

"I'm so fast," Froghat said out loud. "I love this!"

I have to admit, even I was impressed. It was a move I would have made, and I did like seeing the lizardman in great pain. I started to laugh, but then I got a dizzying headache, and things became blurry. "Bring it on," Froghat taunted them. "I can do this all day!"

But the wizard suddenly winced and shook his head, too, as if someone had punched him. He shot me a quick look and muttered, "Uh, oh…"

Both enraged lizardmen pulled back to punch the wizard, and within the blink of an eye, the mind transfer experiment ended, and we were transferred back into our own bodies. I would have been happy about it, but I got back just in time to receive a barrage of punches from the two lizardmen. Beating the wizard senseless would have only taken a second or two, but me? It was going to be awhile.

They both were strong, and the hit's hurt tremendously. "Get em' Gwai Lo!" I heard Froghat yelling from his tree. It was at that point that the lizardmen stopped to catch their breath. "Let's scourge him with the whip," one said between pants. "I bet he won't be so bold then!"

Shaking off the cloudiness of nearly being unconscious, I used my telekinesis to undo the knots in the rope behind me. By the time they reached back with their whips, I had dived forward, clotheslining them both! I tumbled behind them and ended up by where they had stored our gear. Luckily, I was able to grab my magic dagger, Magurk, and hurl it at one of the lizardmen when it got back up. The blade hit him square in the chest, and he sank to his knees before falling to his face in the dirt.

The other one shrieked and ran off into the woods. "My coin!" I yelled. "He's got my coin!"

"Untie us!" the rest of the party cried out as I hurriedly went through our gear, looking for my magic Boots of Speeding.

Frustrated, I stopped looking and ran over to untie the rest of the party. I wanted to leave Froghat tied up, but for some reason, I thought the wizard might be useful in capturing the fleeing lizard-man. "My plan worked out well," Froghat said coolly while I undid his bindings.

"Let's leave all future plans to me," I stated as the ropes fell.

"Look!" hollered Skole, who was now free. "It's the rest of the tribe!"

Coming through the trees, being led by the Chamelion and the wounded lizardman, was a full tribe of the swamp denizens, carrying sharp-looking weapons. "Run!" Stretch Markus shouted. "Let's get to the river!"

Everyone grabbed their gear and took off. I wasn't worried, though; I had my Boots of Speeding, so I quickly slid down and slipped one on. If this didn't give me an advantage over these nincompoops, nothing would. "Ow!" I hollered as I pulled my foot out of my boot.

Something had stung me! When I shook my boot, a small scorpion fell out. Angrily, I crushed it with my fist, grabbed my gear, and began hobbling after the rest. I knew I should have checked them first. That's the first rule of any swampy area! I'd kick myself, but my foot was already starting to swell! I could barely keep up, well, except for Stretch Markus, who was more doing a fast walk while panting heavily. My foot was changing colors, and I knew I had to find one of my poison antidotes, soon!

Dogchauw let out a couple of quick barks, letting us know he found something. When Markus and I finally caught up, the rest of the party was wading out into the Unnamed River. A few yards out was the boat that Froghat and I had used to escape! It was mostly under water and capsized. It would give us an excellent place to hide and hopefully be out of the gaze of the Chamelion.

I sat on a log, shook out both boots, and then put one on. I donned my bandolier, and went into a hidden pocket. Then, I pulled out a poison antidote vial that was a special blend of mine. "Do you want me to suck the poison out of your foot?" Pickenfling asked, staring at the swelling, looking like a deer caught in a Light spell.

"Just get under the boat, you weirdo," I said, frowning. "They are almost here!"

I shoved my other boot in my pack and waded out into the water. Hopefully, soon, I could take the antidote so the swelling would go down, and I could put it back on. I could hear movement in the distance, so I dove under and swam until I could see everyone's legs. When I popped my head above the water, I was inside the overturned boat. "Shhhh…" Froghat whispered, "I can hear them on the shore, talking."

We paddled quietly under the boat for a while, hoping the tribe would lose interest or decide that we went down another path they could investigate. We all hoped it would be soon, because the air under the boat was running out, and we all started feeling light-headed. That's when I noticed an air bubble rise behind Picken-fling. "Was that you?" whispered Froghat. "My-o-my, that is terrible."

Three more bubbles popped up from behind the halfling.

"Are you kidding me?" I whispered angrily, trying not to be sick.

"It's my nerves," Pickenfling whispered back. "This always happens when I'm under a lot of stress!"

Three more large air bubbles rose from behind him and popped when breaking the surface. "See," the halfling said. "Now quit stressing me out!"

The rest of us gagged and tried not to throw up. "I'm going to drown you, you little rat!" I whispered furiously. "But I don't want to move and alert the lizardmen. Would you mind doing it, your-self?!"

More bubbles rose. "Please, Gwai," Stretch Markus whined. "Quit making the little guy nervous, or I'm going to pass out and drown!"

"Shh!" Froghat said softly. "I don't hear anything, now. Ozone is going to check if the coast is clear."

"It ain't clear in here!" Skole whimpered.

Ozone hopped off Froghat's head and into his hand, which he promptly lowered into the water. The wizard raised the frog on the outside of the boat, so its eyes rose above the water. Froghat then began describing what the frog was seeing. "There's only one lizardman on the shore," he began. "It's the one who escaped earlier! He's been left behind to scout from the back. Oh, he's staring at some kind of coin!"

My ears perked up. "I didn't know you could see through Ozone's eyes," I said to Froghat. "Let's go kill that fool!"

"Hold on," Froghat said, closing his eyes and concentrating. "I have a cunning plan."

"Oh, no," I said, "Please, let's just swim over and…"

A muffled fizz went off outside the boat when the wizard mumbled a few words, and then we heard a splash. He turned to me with a grin, "My little Energy Bolt seems to have done the trick!"

I couldn't believe it. The dunderhead killed the lizardman with a spell! We swam to the shore and saw the dead lizardman floating face down at the edge of the water. All the others had left to check for us elsewhere. I tried to swim over faster, but my foot was now killing me, and I felt dizzier than ever; I needed my antidote! I crawled onto the shore and started to convulse. I was able to locate the antidote vial but couldn't raise it to my lips. "Poison… cure…," was all I could mumble.

Pickenfling took the vial from my hand, opened it, and poured it into my mouth. Before I passed out, I heard him start mumbling a healing spell; then all went dark! I woke up an hour later to see everyone milling about. I sat upright and shook my head. "Wow," I said, surprised that they saved me. "I feel much better, now."

"Oh, it was nothing," Pickenfling stated while scratching his armpit. "I just had to hold your mouth open with my fingers to get the vial of antidote in you."

I would have been more disgusted, but then I remembered my coin. I spotted the dead lizardman and ran over to it. I frantically began searching the corpse. "The body has no treasure," remarked Dogchauw. "Skole already took all the goodies off him."

"He what!?" I shouted angrily. "Where is he?"

Pickenfling sniffed his fingertips and grinned. "Oh, he left a few minutes after you passed out," he explained. "He sure was happy about something!"

"Argh!" I shouted, pulling at my hair. "Where did the little crud go? I never got a chance to say goodbye..."

"He went to Miftenmad to join a gang," Pickenfling explained. "He's been wanting to join them for a few years now. They say they are the toughest gang of hoodlums in all of Farlong."

I quickly slipped my remaining boot on, checked my gear, and said, "I gotta run."

"But we were just about to track down the lizardman tribe, come up with another plan, and get that Chamelion," Froghat said. "I want its head mounted on my wall!"

"Good luck with that," was the last thing I said before running off as fast as I could in the direction of Miftenmad.

Chapter 9

I ran for almost an hour before stopping to take a rest. I hadn't seen much, maybe a wild animal or two, but no wandering monsters. I leaned against a tree and rummaged through my gear, looking for my rations. I started to relax a bit after eating a little bread and some dried meat. I took a few gulps from my waterskin and closed my eyes for a minute, letting my stomach settle. That's when I heard the faint sound of music. I quickly gathered my things, activated my Blending Cloak, then headed off in the direction of the sound. Maybe it was a few travelers weighed down by too much gold. So, I figured I better check it out before I continued my search for Skole. I was not happy about the situation with the halfling. Just the sound of his name made me want to spit!

I spotted a covered wagon through the trees. It was slowly making its way through the forest down a trail. On the side of the canvas was painted, "Scales & The Marshtones." "Oh, brother," I mumbled to myself.

This B-Rate band of bards was Froghat's favorite group. I'd hear them at different taverns, once in a while, and each time it would end in a brawl. It's a good thing they had a half-ogre in the group, or they'd never make it out of most places alive! I deactivated my Blending Cloak and walked up. The half-ogre was holding the reins while a human with long, white hair was strumming a lute. He stopped playing the minute he spotted me. The half-ogre frowned and whoa'd the horses. They both eye-balled me suspiciously.

"Are you a fan, robber, or both?" the human asked. "Cuz' Maul here, doesn't like two of the three."

"I'm the associate of a major fan," I explained. "And he would be thrilled to get an autograph."

"He's lying, Peavus," the half-ogre remarked. "Let me smash this rogue!"

"I'm not looking for trouble," I said, holding my hands up. "I was just tracking a halfling when I heard your music."

A lizardman's head popped out between the two, from inside the wagon. "Did somebody say halfling?"

"Calm down, boss," Peavus said, "Remember your diet."

The lizardman frowned, then climbed out of the wagon. Scales was taller than me and walked over as if not worried about me being a threat. "Was this halfling plump at all?" he asked, practically drooling.

"I guess he might have a bit of a belly," I began. "Most halflings do, the way they constantly stuff their faces. This little runt has something of mine, and I want it back."

Scales sniffed the air while the other two climbed out of the wagon. The lizardman then knelt and started smelling. He sniffed the ground and pointed in a northern direction. "He passed through here, alright," Scales said, standing up. "We must have passed him on the way out of Miftenmad."

"So, you saw him?" I asked.

"I didn't see any halfling," Maul said. "But I did wave hello to a scrawny looking dwarf."

"Well, at least I know I'm on the right trail," I said. "Thanks for your help. Could I get an autograph written out to Froghat?"

"Sure thing," Scales said, pulling out a small scroll from his pocket. "We're on our way to Achincorn to play a charity concert. It's for a bunch of lepers; we're raising money for a cure. Tell him he's invited. If he can't make it in time, tell him we're off to Port Laudervale after that."

I watched him autograph the scroll on Peavus's back. "I won't forget," I said, not caring if I did. "I believe Froghat suffers from a rare brain leprosy, so he should fit right in."

It wasn't long before we had parted ways and I was headed toward Miftenmad, once again. Froghat was going to be thrilled with the autograph, and I was going to be thrilled as soon as I opened the small coin purse I lifted off the scaly musician. The bard never realized I snatched it when he handed me the scroll.

As I watched them leave, I waved to the drummer, a ghost who was floating in the back of the wagon. He smiled back and played his ethereal bongos. Froghat said his name was Ghasper and that he was the ghost of a druid who had been killed during a stampede at an Elfis concert. Froghat knew everything about this strange quartet. Apparently, the band never told Ghasper that no one could hear him play unless they were undead and had an attachment to the Plane of Death, where all the undead originate. I usually didn't like druids. I've often said that the only good druid was a dead one. Ghasper fit the bill, so he was okay in my book.

After they left, I checked Scales' coin purse. To my disappointment, all that was in it was a few lute picks, a tour pin, a small vial of scale conditioner, and a recipe for halfling ala mode. I don't know why I ever bother to rob bards.

The rest of the journey to Miftenmad went without incident. The city, as usual, was alive and bustling. Beings from all over Farlong came here to do their shopping and eat at one of its many taverns. Many races embraced diplomacy here and put away normal hatreds, so they could come to play at the jewel of the city, the Dice Tower Tavern. It was there where you could play endless board games, eat junk food, and even gamble the night away, if you so chose. Its recent addition of indoor plumbing didn't hurt, either.

As I walked the streets describing Skole to people, they said they'd only seen a scrawny-looking dwarf with hairy feet. I thanked them after picking their pockets and continued my search. I was getting suspicious about this mystery dwarf and was starting to put two-and-two together when I spotted a bunch of ponies parked in front of the Dice Tower Tavern. I walked up to them and petted one that I recognized. "Just great," I said to myself. "The Black Willow Gang."

I began to wonder if this was the gang that Skole had planned on joining. I would have dismissed this absurd idea altogether, because the Black Willows are all dwarves, but then I remembered the scrawny dwarf with hairy feet! I was beginning to think that Skole was in disguise! I heard a bunch of dwarven laughter as I walked up to the entryway, then I caught the nervous squeaky laugh of a halfling, as well. I paused in front of the door and checked Magurk to make sure it was still in its scabbard. The Black Willows hated my guts, and I had to be mentally and physically prepared to take on whatever would come my way. I would have used my Hat of Disguising, but today I thought I'd take this task head-on. I'd run in, stab Skole, take my coin back, and then make a break for it! I had to admit; my plan was pure genius!

The second I entered the tavern, all conversation stopped, and everyone stopped what they were doing to stare directly at me. I could hear the clock slowly ticking on the wall as I scanned the room. Vasel, the tavern owner, was still polishing a glass and did a small jerk of his head indicating that I should leave, but that fleeting thought was interrupted by the voice of Quade, the leader of the Black Willows. "Well, well, well," the dwarf stated, sliding his chair away from the table, his smile growing quickly. "If it isn't Gwai Lo, the ghost man!"

I grinned back. "I'm not looking for trouble, Quade. I'm just looking for a no-good thief."

"Try looking in the mirror," Quade said menacingly, pointing at me with a crayon he had in his hand. "Oh, are you here looking for this?"

To my shock, he held up my golden Coin of Cheating in his other hand. It flashed as a tavern light reflected off of it. "Do you like it? Our newest member, Skole, gave it to me. He says he beat you up and took it; then you cried like a sissy!"

I looked over, and there was Skole, cowering behind a table. His fake beard disguise was a little twisted off to one side of his face. "I j-j-just said, you were unconscious when I left…"

"Are you kidding me?" I said, pointing at Skole. "He's not even a dwarf!"

Quade raised the crayon, once again. "Are you calling us all liars, ghost man? You don't think I know a dwarf when I see one!?"

Skole adjusted his beard and stepped out from behind the table as the other Black Willows members started forming a circle around me. "Hey guys," Vasel said, coming out from behind the counter. "Let's not get into a brawl, here. Let's settle our differences at the gaming tables."

"Unless, you're afraid," I added.

"He isn't afraid of anything," an ugly dwarf with a spiked helmet chimed in. "Are you, boss?"

"That's right, Pacoyma," Quade said, crossing his arms. "And if this creep doesn't have my Coin of Cheating, there's no way he can win."

"Name the game, baldy," I replied, hoping his lack of hair was a soft spot. "And don't forget to stake your bet."

Quade looked me up and down and said, "If I win, I get your magic dagger. Plus, I get to use it to cut off one of your ears; it's for my collection!"

The crowd gasped as the dwarven gang leader pulled up his beard, revealing his necklace of ears.

"If I win, I get my Coin of Cheating back," I began, "and you have to shave your beard!"

Oooh's could be heard from the crowd, and the dwarf seemed taken aback. "I'll not be shaving my beard for no man," he spit back. "I'd like to see anyone try to enforce that!"

A loud chair scraped as it was pushed backward. From behind a table just around a corner, a large figure appeared. It was Bagbonnet the half-ogre, and she gave me a wink. "You won't be shaving it for a man," she said. "If you lose, you'll be shaving it for me!"

She blew the dwarf a kiss, and Quade looked like he was about to wet himself. On the other hand, Skole suddenly got a sparkle in his eye and blew some air into his palm so he could check his breath. It was apparent the little creep was smitten with the not-so-attractive half-ogre! "Name the game," he softly mumbled as he stepped over to flirt with Bagbonnet.

"All right, all right," Quade stuttered. "How about a game of Scribble?"

"Is that the game where you have to color in the lines?" I asked, knowing that it would be easy.

One of the dwarves immediately stepped over to Quade and whispered in his ear. "What do you mean I can't color, Tuddle?! I'm the best!"

Another one of his gang held up his last drawing. It was a picture of a Centicorn colored in all sorts of ways that are not natural, plus the strokes went way outside the lines. I chuckled as the dwarf's face turned beet red. "Okay, then, wise guy. You pick the game!"

"Can you spell?" I asked.

"You mean like magic or with letters?" Quade replied.

"With letters," I answered.

His men immediately held up their hands and shook their heads, but he ignored them. "Of course, I can," he stated proudly. "I'm the bestest at proper common!"

"Then, let's play Alphabetters," I said smugly. "That should be easy for you. It's just guessing some letters."

I walked over to the table where Quade had been coloring, then pushed the table clear of all its contents; papers and crayons flew everywhere. A crowd gathered around us as we sat on opposing sides of the table. The crowd's murmuring came to a halt as a Black Willow with an eye patch laid a game box on the table between us. I pulled my magic dagger from its scabbard and laid it on the table. Quade then pulled my Coin of Cheating out and held it up. "Let's flip a coin to see who goes first," the dwarf said, smiling.

"I don't think so," I replied. "The instructions say the youngest players should go first."

"That's a dumb human rule!" Quade shouted. "Everyone knows dwarves live longer! It's not our fault you losers snuff it before everyone else!"

The non-humans in the room cheered and laughed in agreement. "Whatever," I replied. "Just play by the rules. I always do."

Thankfully, he didn't see my left hand with fingers crossed behind my back. "Go ahead, let's play this simple game!" he harumphed.

"Now, remember," I said while pulling out the box of question cards. "The first one to get a wrong answer loses the game."

Skole squeezed his way to the front of the table to get a better view and raised an eyebrow at Bagbonnet, who failed to notice the advance. I pulled a card out of the box and cleared my throat. "Ahem," I began. "What is the last letter of the alphabet?"

Quade rubbed his beard for a moment, then started counting his fingers. "Oh, gee, I know this one…" he said out loud.

"Wrong!" I shouted, pounding my fist on the table happily. "It's not 'O' or 'G,' and 1 is a number, you idiot! The answer is 'Z'; you lose!"

The crowd let out a roar, and Quade reached for my dagger, but Bagbonnet slammed him face-first into the table, holding him there. "This outlaw cheated," Quade managed to spit out with his cheek smooshed on the hardwood. "I was just making an expression!"

Bagbonnet then picked him back up off the table, letting him breathe. "Where's my beard, dwarf," she commanded, more than asked. "I want it, now!"

"Take mine, baby!" Skole said, ripping off his fake beard with a grin. "Now, how about a dance!"

After witnessing what they thought was a dwarf ripping off his beard, the dwarves in the room nearly fainted. Except for Quade, who was tossed over a table so the half-ogre could catch the beard flying at her! "Oh, you!" she said, nearly swooning. "What a little charmer!"

Chaos broke out after that as Quade screamed out, "Get that rogue!"

I grabbed my dagger and coin off the table, then jumped out of the way of two dwarves who were diving at me. They hit each other head first before crumpling to the ground. Rolling on the floor, I dodged the grasp of another one. Then I stuck Magurk into his left bottom cheek, which made him scream out like a wizard at a Copper Stop sale! Before I could stand up, the dwarf named Tuddle kicked me in the head with his boot, and it made me go dizzy for a second. Luckily, for me, Bagbonnet was cutting a rug with Skole, and she had swung him around. One of his hairy feet went directly into the dwarf's mouth! When I finally managed to stand up, Quade smashed a chair over my back and sent me crashing over a table and into some customers.

I felt as if the whole event was happening in slow motion. As I fell over the table, knocking game pieces everywhere, I saw my Coin of Cheating go flying away from me while I crashed into the gamers, who were now screaming out in surprise. "You ruined our game," they yelled from the floor over the chairs that had been destroyed.

They were still hollering about something as I reached out for their short, chubby half-orc friend who had stood up and was holding the coin. "Whoa," he stated, "Thank you!"

Quade and I looked at each other, then back at the half-orc. "He's got the coin!" we both yelled.

With a squeal, the half-orc ran out the front door while Quade and I stumbled over broken pieces of the table as we tried to do the same. "I'm putting the damage on your tabs!" yelled out Vasel, as we both kicked the doors open and fled out onto the street.

We both spotted the fleeing creature take off on his horse into the woods around the side of a building. Quade tripped me by throwing a broken off table leg, causing me to land on my face. "So long, chump!" he laughed while jumping on his pony and kicking its sides.

The smile on his face did not last long, though. I had used some rope to tie all the pony's legs together when I first got there. When his pony tried to run, it collapsed, sending Quade flying face-first into the dirt. "Sorry, fella," I said, patting his stunned pony, before delivering a knock out kick to its owner's face.

Wiping blood from my nose, I took a deep breath, then took off after the half-orc at full throttle.

Chapter 10

Even with my Boots of Speeding on and running at breakneck speed, I was struggling to keep up with the half-orc's horse. The ugly culprit knew how to ride it, too! He weaved the animal around the trees of the forest without looking back at all. I was feeling confident, though. That half-orc had no idea how tenacious I could be, especially when pursuing something I cared about! I thought about shooting him in the back with my Swatfly bow, but that meant I would have to stop running to aim, and I didn't want him getting that far ahead.

The horse ran up and over a sharp incline and flew into the air, while the half-orc yelled, "Yee-haw!"

I also made the leap. The horse masterfully hit the ground running and took a curve down the trail, nearly skidding out on some loose soil. On the other hand, I landed into a tumbling roll, then popped back up with no problem. I almost skidded out, as well, but managed to keep my footing. My target was only a few yards ahead, now.

Trying to shake me, the half-orc made the horse jump a tree that had fallen over. I opted to slide underneath an opening at its base. Unfortunately for me, my cloak got caught on one of its gnarled branches, and I had to stop and untangle myself. When I restarted my run, I spotted my target off in the distance. I almost got up to full speed, again, but what I saw next took me by surprise. A giant hand lowered itself from above the trees and grabbed the horse and rider! I hit the brakes and slid a few feet before ducking behind a tree. "What in the realms?" I whispered between panting breaths. That's when I took note of my surroundings. Up above the tree line, I could see the Hoktu Mountains, which could only mean one thing, giants!

I had a bad feeling as I approached the area where the hand had snatched my prize away. I caught the faint odor of something foul, and I could see a light green mist floating in the air. It had to be a fog giant, the largest breed of them all! The huge beings liked to eat other creatures, one piece at a time. I waited to catch my breath and began to saunter ahead, making sure not to crunch any fallen leaves or twigs. I also activated my Cloak of Blending before moving to where I saw the horse and rider disappear. "Please don't let the giant be Zham Leaf," I mumbled, hopefully.

I had many run-ins with this vicious fog giant in the past. Zham Leaf hated me with a passion, and to be honest; the feeling was mutual. I'd rather lick a wart covered scab than to deal with this oversized potato brain. I could see where the giant had pushed the trees apart, so the trail was not hard to spot. As quietly as I could, I tiptoed my way along the new path. The crushed vegetation was helpful, but it didn't matter that much. The thing about fog giants is that you just followed your nose if you wanted to find them. Within moments I could see heavier green fog lingering in the air. I knew I was close when I heard humming. It would stop momentarily, then begin again.

As I daringly stepped closer, I could see the giant sitting in a cleared-out patch of the woods. It was indeed, my dreaded foe, Zham Leaf. I let out a quiet sigh and looked at his ugly, scarred face. "Please don't eat my coin, please don't eat my coin," I mumbled to myself in horror as I could see Zham Leaf pull a leg off his screaming victim.

The smiling giant gingerly popped it into his mouth! The half-orc holloered out for mercy but I knew it would come. Personally, I wouldn't wish this death upon anybody, except for maybe Onquay, Apichat, Elfalfuh, Quade, and a long list of others. I snuck a few feet further before Zham placed the upper half of his victim into his mouth and crunched down, biting his writhing snack in half, leaving only his bottom and one flopping leg.

I guess he truly was a half-orc, now! I leaned against a tree, considering my next move while the ugly giant happily munched his meal. Zham held the panicking horse in his other hand. I was feeling frustrated. How was I supposed to get my Coin of Cheating back, now? Did he just swallow it? Was I prepared to follow him around for days with a shovel, hoping it would pass through him quickly? The thought turned my stomach.

"Mmmm, boney," the giant commented while chewing the legs.

Zham Leaf patted his belly and let out a loud belch. To my amazement, when he smiled, I could see the half-orc's hand stuck between two of the giant's rotting teeth, and it was still holding my coin! He smacked his lips a couple of times, then reached into his mouth to pull out one of the half-orc's leg bones, with which he proceeded to pick his teeth. I padded a few yards closer when the bone finally managed to work the hand free. The makeshift toothpick flung it out of the giant's mouth before it hit the ground with a small thud. I could see the bloodied coin, and it wasn't that far from me!

"Now for dessert," Zham Leaf commented as he held up the horse, which was kicking like crazy. "Heads or tails, hmmm, where me begin?"

The giant took a minute and took a big sniff of the horse, as if to savor the aroma. That's when his face froze, and he raised an eyebrow. He lowered the horse and sniffed again. "Dragonbait?" he stated. "Dragonbait, is that you?"

I hated when he called me that. It brought back the not-so-fond memory of when he used me as a lure to catch young dragons to eat. I could still feel the pain in my leg when two Bjinsford dwarves had rescued me with an incredibly sharp arrow. I shook off the thought and ran over and grabbed the hand still clutching my coin. While I ran, the giant leaned over, releasing more green fog. The blast had me stumble back a bit, and I tripped over a fallen log.

Zham Leaf laughed as he sat the horse down and reached for me. He caught the back of my Blending Cloak and lifted me off the ground with no effort at all. The giant held me up to his face and smiled. I deactivated my cloak and hung there, helpless. "How in the realms did you see me?" I asked, hoping to stall the buffoon. "I should have been invisible to you!"

"Me could see your shape in my fog," he laughed menacingly. "You not very smart, are you Dragonbait?"

As you could probably guess, my mind was racing, trying to figure out a way out of the predicament. "I wouldn't say that," I began. "You see, my party is not far behind me, and they kill giants, just for fun!"

Zham Leaf frowned and took a quick peek over the treetops. Then, he sniffed a few times before stating, "Bah haha! You take me for giant fool!"

"Yes," I said, crossing my arms. "I do! And your momma wears large wombat boots!"

The giant stood up quickly with a look of amusement, "Just wait until she sees you!"

I didn't know who he was talking about, perhaps he was thinking of taking me to his mother. I had to think fast. "You don't scare me, giant. My party has an all-powerful wizard named Froghat, who always has a plan!"

"Froghat? That sound dumb," Zham Leaf said. "Like he wears frog on head."

Then, I stretched out my arms. "Our cleric is Pickenfling," I continued, trying to frighten him. "He is so frightening; even I don't want to be around him!"

The giant paused, like he was starting to believe me. "Don't get me started on Stretch Markus the Brave," I continued. "He eats danger like it's an all-you-can-eat buffet, and he always comes back for more! And don't think you can escape, either, because Dogchauw the Ferocious will hunt you down, no matter where you run! So, if I were you, I'd just let me go before they figure out what happened."

The giant stayed quiet for a moment, mulling over my words. "Me not scared. Methinks you lie."

"All right, then, I hope you packed a lunch, cuz' this is going be a long scrap!" I threatened.

"Don't worry, Dragonbait. You'll not be eaten…yet," he stated before gripping me tightly in his hand and then turning toward the Hoktu Mountains. "First, me got big surprise for you."

I sighed, but had no choice but to go along. At least I had my coin back, so that was a plus. As I was carried across the forest, I thought of Froghat and the gang. I figured that they were all hacked apart by lizardmen, by now, or being slowly digested by the

Chamelion. With my luck lately, I'd probably step into a pile of what's left of them and then have to have my boots cleaned. Or maybe they strode boldly into the camp, killed all the monsters, and would be celebrating their glorious victory!

"What you laughing at, Dragonbait?" the giant said after hearing my inadvertent chuckle. "What so funny?"

"Oh, nothing," I said, wishing that I could reach Magurk, which I could feel being tightly squeezed into my side.

After a half-hour of walking, we reached the base of the Hoktu Mountains, and he started climbing. Even one-handed, I was impressed at Zham Leaf's skills. At least I was still alive, for the moment. I found the cooler air at this height refreshing. Flecks of snow appeared, here and there, as we ascended. I managed to take a couple of deep breaths when I could, so that I didn't pass out from the thinner air at that height. In my light-headed state, I thought about different areas I might stab the giant. Maybe I could find a weak spot and kill him, somehow. I looked all over him, but nothing stood out, other than his ugly mug. Before I could ponder the situation further, Zham Leaf slipped inside a cave in the side of the mountain.

It was large, messy, and surprise, surprise, quite smelly. Bones, bits of fur, and a few giant feathers were strewn around. There was also a beat-up looking cage made of bones. But, what caught my attention the most, was a mostly decomposed body of a female fog giant leaning against a wall. "This be my new girlfriend; her name is Kayto," Zham Leaf boasted. "Me let her decide what to do with you!"

"Um, you know she's dead, right?" I said as he dangled me in front of her. "I think you hear voices in your head!"

"Quiet, Dragonbait," Zham Leaf stated, giving me a little shake. "Hello, Kayto. Me brought us some lunch, me love."

To my shock, a small voice came from the rotting skull of the corpse! "Oh, he's a scrawny one! Did you bring anything more?"

"What is this?!" I yelled out. "Some kind of magic?!"

"Our love is what keeps me alive," Kayto replied. "Now, hush up, rogue!"

Zham Leaf looked at me, smugly. Then, sat me into the cage made from bones. He sat a giant rock over the top opening to keep me from escaping. "Don't worry, love. Me go get us more!"

With that said, he ran out to the edge and clambered back down from the entrance. I couldn't believe I was stuck here with some weird type of giant talking zombie. Not wanting to be trapped, I shook the bone bars, but they held fast. I used my Ring of Spider Climbing to crawl up to the top and noticed a gap that I hoped I could get through. "Do you see a way out?" Kayto's voice spoke. "Can you make it?"

"What's it to you?" I replied. "Won't you just grab me and eat me as I try to escape?"

The giant zombie voice laughed. "Of course not, Gwai Lo. I need you to help me!"

I was perplexed that the undead creature knew my nickname. Without further hesitation, I squeezed my way through the gap like a halfling dancer at an overweight dance contest. Within moments, I was free. I checked my pocket for the Coin of Cheating and made my way toward the edge of the opening of the cavern. "Wait," cried Kayto's voice. "Don't leave me here; I'm stuck!"

"How do you know me?" I asked, turning to face the weird creature.

"We went to school together, you nitwit!" she said with un-moving lips. "I need your help, because I'm stuck inside this skull!"

"Kellepto?" I said, suddenly remembering the voice. "Kayto, Kellepto. Oh, I get it, he butchered your name!"

"He'll butcher both of us sooner or later if we don't get out of here!" she remarked. "But you've got to help me!"

I quickly climbed up the corpse and pushed some dried flesh aside around the cheekbone. Once in the skull, I could see the beautiful elf I used to have a crush on leaning against what looked like a giant prune. "It's the giant's dried-up brain," Kellepto said, patting it. "Pretty small for a creature so big, eh?"

I laughed. "That doesn't surprise me."

Walking up to her, I could see Kellepto's leg was broken in at least two places, and it was swollen. "Please tell me you have a Potion of Healing or something," she said, wincing in pain. "I've been here for two days, and I don't think I can take much more!"

Thankfully, Zham Leaf hadn't crushed any of the secret vials hidden in my cloak. I just happened to have one last Potion of Healing I kept for emergencies. I handed her the vial, and she quickly gulped it down. Within moments, the leg adjusted itself and shrank back to its normal size. Kellepto quickly jumped at my pack and started digging through it. "Hey, watch it, woman!" I said, trying to get her off my back.

"Sorry," she said, pulling out a handful of dried bread, which she stuffed into her mouth. "I was starving!"

I crossed my arms and smiled as she ate. It was nice seeing my old classmate, again, even under weird circumstances like this. "So, of all the giant rotting skulls in this world, why did I stumble into yours?" I joked.

"Haha," she smirked. "Very funny."

I handed her my waterskin, and she drank deeply, then let out a small belch. "I was scouting ahead for my party and decided to do a little bit of climbing to survey the area," she explained. "Then, I saw this place and wanted to investigate."

She pulled out a handful of nice-looking gems. "Not a bad haul, eh?"

I was impressed, maybe a little too much, it seemed, because she quickly tucked them away after seeing my widening grin. "I was just about to leave when I got attacked by a Driderman that happened to find the place, as well. I managed to cut him deep, but not before he smashed me in the leg a couple of times with his club."

Dridermen were a creature that I despised. Their bottom half was that of a giant spider and their top half was usually an overly hairy man. They loved to wear gaudy necklaces and brag about themselves to Driderwomen. They were also incredibly deadly and loved to drink the blood of most other races. I have heard about groups of them even taking down fog giants!

Kellepto peeked outside the skull to see if the coast was clear. "Luckily for me, I was able to climb into this fog giant's corpse and hide from the Dridermen. If they could drain this one dry, I'd hate to see what they would have done to me!"

"So Zham Leaf found you and fell in love," I chuckled. "What a maroon!"

"Hey," Kellepto warned with a grin. "I remember you and Aggression giving me the eye."

"That's because you always had gold," I said, pushing my way out through the cheekbone, again. "My only true weakness!"

The elf climbed down behind me and we raced to the entrance. Just as we reached the edge, a Driderman flew over our heads and splatted on the back wall of the cavern before sliding down with a dull thud. "Hide," I told Kellepto while quickly taking off my magic cloak and throwing it over her.

She backed off just as Zham Leaf's head appeared before me. "Me brought more food, my love ..hey, Dragonbait. How did you escape cage?!"

I backed up as the giant entered and grabbed me, once again. I hoped Kellepto had a plan, because I was undoubtedly in a jam, or would soon be mashed into some! The giant snatched up the dead Driderman with his other hand and brought us over to the corpse of Kayto. "A romantic feast for two!" he declared, before popping off the dead driderman's head and trying to feed it to Kayto like a grape.

Zham Leaf's expression changed from a romantic grin to a look of concern. "Kayto?" he stated before giving her a nudge.

The corpse fell forward and crashed onto the floor. That's when the head rolled off and into a corner. The fog giant looked shocked as he watched the skull come to a full rest before looking down at me with a look of rage! "You killed her! Now, me going to kill you!"

I was just about to protest when the fog giant let out a "yelp." To my amazement, I saw a half-dozen Dridermen crawling over his body and plunging their stingers into him. Zham Leaf dropped the dead Driderman and I and started smacking at the hairy-chested arachnids attacking him. "Foul pests!" he cried out, as one burst into goo under his fist.

70

Tumbling to the floor, I did my best to dance around the giant's feet, which were moving all over the place. I wasn't worried about the Dridermen; they all seemed to be focused on getting revenge for their fallen comrade. Before I knew it, Kellepto appeared out of nowhere and handed me my cloak. "We've got to get out of here, fast!" she yelled over the cries of the creatures in combat.

"I have an idea!" I said, running over to the skull of the dead giant; it wobbled when I touched it.

"You are insane!" she shouted. "There's no way I'm getting back into that!"

Just then, we both watched Zham Leaf rip a Driderman in half and scream with rage as he looked down at us. "I'm in!" she shouted, changing her mind rather suddenly.

We rolled the skull to the edge of the cave, and both climbed in. The fog giant tried to move toward us, but the venom from the Dridermen was making him dizzy. When another Driderman crawled over his face, he threw it to the ground and stepped on it, mashing its guts out onto the cave floor. "They aren't going to last long against him!" I shouted to Kellepto. "Let's rock!"

We immediately began to rock the skull forward and backward, trying to get it rolling. "Dragonbait!" I heard the giant scream out in a gurgle.

At the same time, I heard another Driderman scream out in pain. "Hurry!" I yelled, rocking the skull with all my might.

When it fully rolled, Kellepto and I jumped into an eye socket and grabbed the dried brain, holding on for dear life! I got a hollow feeling in my stomach as the skull toppled over the edge and entered a free fall. I closed my eyes for a moment to absorb the strange feeling. It only lasted a second, though, as the skull hit the slope of the mountain and began to roll at an incredible speed! Kellepto and I were forced against the inside wall of the skull. We were spinning around and around as we tumbled downward. I could have sworn I heard Zham Leaf's voice in the distance yelling, "Come back, Kayto! Come back!"

Kellepto and I yelled, too, as we rolled down the mountain at top speed. I thought I would be sick, but I noticed the skull leveling off after a short bit, and then I heard it smack off a tree and bounce us in a horizontal position. We had slowed a little, well, at least enough to see that we were rolling past some trees and possibly across an open plain. "Nimbus!" Kellepto cried out as we passed what appeared to be a group of adventurers.

They yelled out her name, too, but we had rolled by too fast to respond. I was just about to give up hope, but after a few minutes, we stopped moving, I heard a splash, and water sprayed in on us. We both crumpled to the bottom and could feel the water coming in, quickly. I was so dizzy that I couldn't stand, but I splashed water on my face to shake the nausea. I could see that Kellepto was doing the same thing, as well. When the water was up to our knees, we climbed out of the skull and onto its top. "Lake Underglub," I panted, squinting in the sunlight. "We made it!"

The fog giant's skull was sinking fast, so we both decided to dive into the water and swim for the shore. It didn't seem that far, but in the condition that we were, it was a real chore! At long last, we made it to the shoreline and collapsed face-first in the sand. "You certainly know how to keep a girl entertained," Kellepto laughed while rolling onto her back.

I just giggled and stood up, still feeling a bit shaky. "Hey," I replied, still catching my breath. "That's just how I roll."

"Here," Kellepto said, holding out her hand. "For your trouble."

She dropped a couple of gems from the bag into my hand. I held an emerald up to the sunlight. The green light was beautiful. "Nice," I said. "You sure have an eye for gemstones."

"Kellepto!" a voice cried out in the distance. "Kellepto!"

"Over here!" she yelled back. "Nimbus! We're over here!"

She turned to me. "You're going to like Nimbus. He's the most honest and lawfully good paladin in all the realms."

"Awful good is more like it," I commented to myself.

I was a wanted man in almost all of the realms; from angry villagers to kings, themselves, I always seemed to be in trouble for something. So, I wasn't too keen on having any lawman within spitting distance. When Kellepto ran forward to meet Nimbus, I activated my cloak that she had returned and padded off behind a tree.

"There you are!" Nimbus said, running up to Kellepto, picking her up for a bear hug.

Her arms dangled at her sides as she squeaked, "I'm okay, I'm okay!'

The red-bearded human was just over seven feet tall and carried a deadly looking claymore. "That skull you were riding in ran right over Footpalm!" he said, setting her down gently.

The rest of her party came running up, huffing and puffing. A skinny cleric was helping a dwarf who looked like he'd seen better days. "Aye," the bald dwarf stated. "You smashed me well!"

"Sorry about that," Kellepto said. "A rotting fog giant skull is not known for its steering capabilities! We barely survived!"

"We?" said a goofy looking wizard. "Who's we?"

Kellepto looked around. I could tell she now recognized that I didn't want to be seen. She knew of my aversion to lawmen who couldn't be bought. "It's a long story, Garrot," she sighed. "Can we go get something to eat?"

"Yes!" the paladin triumphantly shouted as they walked off. "Food fixes everything!"

Kellepto threw an over-the-shoulder wave in my direction as I stepped out to watch them walk off. I looked at the gems in my hand and smiled. My boots were still squishing with wetness as I started walking in the direction of Neverspring. The sun was out, and I hoped that all my wet clothes would dry quickly.

Chapter 11

It felt good to have my coin back, yet again. As I gripped it in my hand I began to wonder about why, all of a sudden, it kept getting separated from me. It almost felt like some kind of curse, at that point. I started to get angry when I thought about Schmendrake distracting me, causing me to drop it in the first place! This whole thing was his fault, and I thought about paying him a special visit when I got back.

The thoughts left my mind as I felt the warm sun on my face. It was getting to be late afternoon and I was enjoying my casual stroll back to Neverspring. Then, I remembered that I should pick up my pace. After all, Bub and Lar were trusting me to guard the Palm Eye Finger Magic Shop. I could probably run the whole way in five or six hours, but I just didn't feel like running, anymore. That roll down the Hoktu Mountains had put a strain on my equilibrium and I was still feeling a little dizzy.

I was heading northeast and knew I'd be getting close to the city of Humderum soon. The place wasn't very exciting, but they did have a tavern that I liked called the Fish Udder. I was starving and I tended to enjoy everything on the menu there, except the milk. There was just something fishy about it.

As I walked into town, I couldn't believe my eyes. There was a lot more hustle and bustle than there had been before. Humanoids of every type were milling about, going to shops, haggling with street vendors, or just going about their business. I even spotted the wagon of Wellhoff the Minotaur, but I avoided him and ducked down an alley. Not that there was anything to fear from him; after all, I helped him get his prize product, Flying Bull, out into market. I was just afraid he'd pull me back into the snake oil business, which was much too dishonest for my liking. I liked to earn coin the old-fashioned way; by pinching it off others when they weren't paying attention!

When I arrived at the Fish Udder Tavern, I could see that the place was much busier. I found a seat up at the counter and ordered something with chicken in it. "Good choice," stated the human next to me. "The chicken here is to die for."

He was a creepy-looking bloke with eyes that bugged out and went in differing directions. His scraggly orange hair hung to his shoulders and his eyebrows seemed to have grown together. He was dressed like a rogue, but he could have been another class, I just couldn't put my finger on it. "Good, because I'm starving," I said, after turning back to look at the menu.

I pretended to read it while the goofball kept talking to me. I ignored him for the most part, but then he asked me where I was

74

going. "To Neverspring," I replied. "I've got a job to do."

"Me too!" the man declared happily. "Need a fellow rogue to help you out? I'm very sneaky and I blend right into a crowd."

I highly doubted that, because his one eye did a weird roll when he said this. This clown would stick out like a Garbarian at a clothing shop! "My name is Dunfer. Rogue for hire," he said happily, holding out his hand.

I ignored the handshake attempt, but did notice the nice-look- ing magic ring he wore. My lich eye always helped me spot items like this, because anything magical would glow with a slight blue tinge. "Thanks for the offer," I said, "But I work alone. Besides, it's a long walk."

"Why walk," Dunfer replied. "Why not use Humderum's new lairport?"

"So, that's why the city has grown?" I asked, more to myself than him.

"Oh, yes," he smiled. "And there's more opportunity for, you know, roguery!"

Lairports were the hottest thing in the realms at the time. New ones were popping up all over the place, opening up travel and bringing in business to small towns like Humderum. Dragons lined their backs with seats that passengers could board and then they would fly them to their destination. The downside was that dragons would gobble up customers, occasionally, but that was kind of rare, so most people didn't mind taking the risk.

I felt the gems in my pocket, so I knew I could cover the cost of the ticket. Besides, I could pick a couple of pockets on my way out of the lairport in Neverspring to recoup the money. I paid for my food and excused myself from the talkative rogue. "Perhaps we'll meet again?" Dunfer asked, almost pleadingly, as I left.

I gave a wave from over my shoulder and was glad to be out of there. I had debated on stealing his ring, but even though he an- noyed me, I rather felt sorry for him, because of his homely appear- ance. He should have been a wizard or something, so he could cast blind spells on any women he'd like to meet! I walked out the door of the tavern, stopped at a dwarven bread vendor, and asked for directions to the lairport. It was only a few blocks away, so I ducked into an alley and donned my magic Hat of Disguising, making myself look like a friendly cleric. I figured, why walk about looking like a rogue when you can get closer to people as your friendly, neighborhood healer man.

Along the walk to the lairport, I would inadvertently, wink wink, bump into richer looking people and lighten their gold burdens a bit. "Pardon me," I'd laugh with a friendly smile.

When I got to the outside gate of the lairport I almost got run over by an overweight elf gal carrying a few bags of luggage.

"Foolish cleric," she seethed. "Can't you see I'm in a hurry!"

"I apologize ma'am," I replied, slipping a few gold coins into my pocket that I lifted off of her.

"Humpfh," she snorted back. "All you clerics do is pass the plate!"

"I don't think you've passed too many," I'd replied with the tip of the hat.

"What did you say?" she asked sharply.

"I said, if there's a good cause, how can you just pass by?" I lied. "It just so happens that I have a charity called Mice, Elf, and Eye. It's all about helping blind rodents to see again by using elf magic. Would you care to donate?"

She rolled her eyes. "I guess," she griped. "Anything to keep you bothersome clerics out of my hair. That's why I left Neverspring! Did you know there was some big cleric whoop-dee-doo there two nights ago?"

All of a sudden, I recognized her as the lady I had run into while chasing my coin. I was glad that I had on my Hat of Disguising. "And to make things worse, I got my bottom stuck in a sewer grate after trying to catch a thief!"

I just smiled as she handed me a couple gold coins. "Hmm, I thought I had more than this," she said, while dropping her remaining coins back into her pocket. "Oh well. At least I'm away from all that mess, good day, sir!"

"Mice, Elf, and Eye thank you," I said, as I turned toward the entrance.

She paused for a moment, as if she almost realized something. Then, she shook her head and walked off. I patted the gold in my pocket and whistled all the way to the ticket booth. There, I purchased a one-way ticket to Neverspring. Sure, it cost me the smaller of the two gems, but it would be worth it. I just wanted to relax and enjoy the view. I almost walked right up to the gate, but then realized they would use a scan spell on me and ruin my disguise. Thus, I went into a stall in the men's room and removed the Hat of Disguising. Then, I hustled back to the gate.

"Are you wearing weapons?" the bored looking security wizard asked, as she ran a Detection Wand over me.

"Of course," I said.

"Any explosives? Or a dragon killing lance?" she asked.

"No," I replied.

"I need you to take off your boots," she stated. "And wait over there."

"Ugh," I groaned. "You're not a Bog Wizard, are you?"

"Just doing my job," she said, lifting my boot to her nose, giving it a big sniff, and smiling.

Angrily, I marched barefoot over to the area where we were supposed to wait. I hated all the rigermarole that you were forced to go through at lairports, just to fly on a dragon. "Bunch of boot lickers," I mumbled, watching her run her tongue along the soles of my Boots of Speeding.

Eventually, my gear was returned and I marched to the ramp that led up to the back of the big green dragon that was to fly me to Neverspring. The giant winged lizard just laid there snoozing while a stewardess led people to their seats. When she finally got to me, she said, "Welcome to Flight 815, your dragon's name is Slipshod. Let me show you to your seat."

"Can I get one that's not over a wing," I asked, when I climbed the ramp.

"Sure thing," the stewardess smiled, guiding the way. "What is your seat number?"

"7A," I said, showing her my ticket.

"That's got a great view," she said, giving me a wink. "No need to shuffle seats around."

The stewardess led the way and I sat down in the cramped seat, but I was happy I had a nice view off the side. "Make sure to buckle in," she reminded me. "We'd hate to lose such a handsome customer."

The stewardess smiled and I grinned in return. Then, I tilted my chair back and closed my eyes. I was hoping to get in a little nap before take-off. I had no such luck as I heard a loud voice, just as I was about to doze off. "What do you mean I can't sit next to my wife?!" a deep baritone hollered. "Then, just where do I sit?!"

I opened my eyes to see an extremely large, balding man in a flowered tunic staring in my direction with a frown. "Please don't let it be here, please don't let it be here," I kept repeating to myself.

Naturally, it was to no avail. The stewardess led him over and he begrudgingly squeezed his ample frame into the seat next to me. The stewardess gave me a sad look, as if to say I'm sorry, and I gave her an understanding look back. I was forced to lean to my left so one of his belly rolls didn't crush my right arm. It was obvious that he was trying to mask his body odor with some cologne, but it honesty didn't help much.

"We're in the seats behind you, Morby," his wife said, as she and their son took their places.

Morby must have been rich, because his wife was a real knock-out, and could have been a model. Their young son, on the other hand, looked like a miniature version of his father; overweight, and even balding! I wondered how much money this big oaf had on him at that moment. "You don't mind if I snack, do you?" he said turning to me, holding a large chunk of crumble cake.

I shook my head and he happily ate, as crumbles fell off with each bite, rolled down his chins, and fell all over me. I sighed and closed my eyes, hoping for sleep. "Could this flight get any worse?" I mumbled to myself.

That's when I heard the screams of a bunch of toddlers. "Fine, you can all sit on my lap!" screamed out a familiar voice.

Curious, I stood up and peered a few rows back before quickly ducking back down in my seat and pulling my hood over my face.

The man was Gerbernoob the Wizard, and he had all the Patterlings with him. He looked terrible, as always. I didn't know why he was flying, but I hoped that he would not notice me. If I kept low and used the big guy as a blocker, I could get away with not having to hear a sob story from the worn out old spellcaster.

"We are now ready for take-off," said the pretty stewardess, standing between the two aisles of seats. "Now, if everyone can look up here while I give flight instructions."

She moved her hands over her waist. "Now make sure you keep your safety belt on at all times," she began. "Please make sure you stay in your seats until after takeoff. Once we reach the proper altitude, you are allowed only to remove them for a bathroom break. There are two enclosed chamberpots in the back that are securely attached. Our dragon, Slipshod, ate a healthy lunch just before his nap, so I am highly confident that this flight will go smoothly, with no digestinal turbulence."

After buckling herself in, she blew on a whistle signaling Slipshod that we were ready for takeoff. He let out a quick roar to let the other dragons in the lairport know he was about to walk over to the departure gate. With another roar, the dragon launched itself into the air. Within seconds, we passed through the clouds. "Neverspring, here we come!" shouted Morby to his family.

I watched the clouds passing gently below us and nodded out. The wind felt great and it was just warm enough that I could feel at ease. I dreamed of sleeping face first in a large, soft pillow. I would like to say that nothing could have woken me, but I was startled awake when I heard a loud scream! Disoriented, I pulled my face from the pillow and realized it wasn't a pillow at all, but a roll of Morby's fat, and I had drooled on his tunic! Frantic, I stood up and started wiping my face and spitting. "Does anyone have any potions of Cure Grossness?"

I looked down at Morby who had fallen asleep, as well. Behind him, his wife was holding her a finger to her lips to shush me while pointing at something.

"I said, don't anybody move!" yelled out a familiar voice above the din of shrieks. "Hey! It's the outlaw!"

When my eyes focused, I could see Dunfer standing in the middle of the aisle holding a lance for killing dragons. It was pointed directly at Slipshod's spine. "I decided to do a robbery, a hijacking, and maybe some killing, too! Great plan, eh?"

"What are you going to do Dunfer, kill the dragon? It will crash and we'll all die!" I said, trying to reason with him. "Let's just get to Neverspring, and then you and I can pick a few pockets. What do you say?"

Dunfer turned to the cowering stewardess, "Tell this ugly beast to fly us to Dociletoff, and make it snappy!"

"There's nothing in Dociletoff," I stated. "Just a bunch of peanut farmers."

"I'll take my chances," he said, raising his only eyebrow. "So, the first demand is that everyone start filling this large sack with their valuables. Starting with...um, you!"

He pointed a finger at Gerbernoob. The old wizard appeared frightened, for a moment, then a big smile crossed his face. "Yes!" He hollered, nearly rising out of his seat. "I mean, shucks, all I have is this box of ultra-valuable gems!"

I knew the gems determined who the Patterlings would cling to, and I saw the restrained grin on the wizard's face when he placed the box into the sack that Dunfer had tossed at him. I just shook my head. Boy, was Dunfer in for a shock when he realized that the Patterlings would be tied to him day and night, without any relief, whatsoever. He was probably going to learn the hard way that Patterlings are also indestructible. The old witch who made the creatures had discovered powerful magical gems, which she bound them to.

I watched as Gerbernoob leaned back in his seat with his hands behind his head. He knew that the minute this hijacking lunatic opened the box to claim it, the Patterlings would now be that fool's problem!

"How did you sneak that lance aboard?" I asked the crazed rogue. "I mean, they politely ask you if you have one before you get on board."

"I lied," Dunfer laughed. "Plus, this is magical. It collapses in on itself, so you can tuck it away."

"There goes Neverspring," the stewardess said, pointing to the north. "We should be in Dociletoff in a half hour."

That's when Morby woke up. "What's with all the noise? I was having a good dream about a beautiful maiden nibbling at one of my rolls!"

"This guy's hijacking the dragon, and I don't think he's willing to negotiate" I whispered, pointing at Dunfer. "There goes our in-flight meal…"

I knew this would set Morby off, but I didn't think he'd go absolutely bonkers! "Give me your weapon, rogue!" he said, grabbing at the hilt of my dagger. "I'll kill this buffoon!"

I twisted away from the grab and the rotund man wrestled with me, trying to take it. I went to move him away, but he crushed me with his girth, knocking the wind out of me. Morby grabbed Magurk and ran off in the direction of Dunfer. By the time I regained my breath, I saw Morby swing my dagger at the rogue, forcing his target to dodge the swings. Then, Dunfer angrily plunged the lance into the dragon's back! With a screech, Slipshod lurched in the air and a couple of passengers flew off into the clouds. Luckily, for the stewardess, I was able to grasp her hand before she would have flown off, as well. "Hold on!" I hollered as I held on to the back of my seat.

The dragon was descending at a high-velocity and people quit screaming as they clenched their teeth, just trying to hang on. I could hear the giggles of the Patterlings as they thought this was all a huge game! I also saw Gerbernoob holding the loot bag and crawling up the aisle, clinging onto seats. He was trying to give the bag to Dunfer! He really was desperate! Dunfer screamed at Morby, "You fool! You're ruining everything!"

The rogue was kicking Morby in the face, trying to get him to let go, but the large man was determined. "You're done for, rogue, give it up!" he hollered, before stabbing Dunfer in the leg, who screamed out like banshee. "I paid for an in-flight meal and I'm going to have it!"

Dunfer could not stop the larger man. Morby grabbed the

lance and pulled it most of the way out of the dragon's spine. The large creature let out a gasping breath and leveled out a little, but blood was flowing out quite heavily. We were still coasting at a high rate of speed and I could see we were only a couple of hundred feet above the ground. It was obvious that we were gliding over the Barrendry desert, just north of the rocky craigs and mesas.

No longer being in a deep dive, Gerbernoob saw his chance and jumped at Dunfer, trying to force the sack into his hands, "Take my gems! Take my gems!"

The rogue almost took them, but Morby gave the hijacker a punch to the face that knocked him back into the lance, driving if farther down. This made Slipshod tilt to one side and Gerbernoob lost his grip, slipped on some blood, and fell off the dragon to the desert sand below. Each Patterling disappeared in a blink, that's how I knew the wizard probably survived the fall. The wizard might have used a Falling Feather spell. Or, he's just lying in the sand, extremely injured, with dancing, unsympathetic Patterlings all around.

Before I could react, Morby had made his way back to the lance and successfully pulled it out of the dragon's back. The giant lizard was woozy, now, and only barely flying above the ground. At least it leveled off. Cheers erupted from the other passengers, but Dunfer was not too happy about it. He let out a scream, and with the last of his strength, tackled Morby, sending them both over the side of the dragon!

I screamed "Nooooo!" as I watched the two go overboard, with my magical dagger.

Luckily for me, Slipshod had been flying over a small lake, just north of the mesas. I didn't hesitate to dive off the side in hot pursuit! I splashed into the water without too much of an impact. I went quite deep, but managed to break above the top to look around.

To the north of me was vegetation, and to the south, was the edge of the Barrendry desert. I had no idea where Dunfer and Morby went, but I assumed that, if they survived, they would have gone to the north. So, I slowly began the swim. By the time that I had gotten to the shore, I was exhausted and had to lay there a little while to catch my breath. I could not believe I ended up in this predicament, twice in one day!

I knew it was going to be dark in a few hours, so I jumped up and scanned the area, looking for bodies in the water or footprints along the shoreline. What I spotted next killed any hope of survival that I had. It was multiple Centicorn tracks, heading toward Docile-toff. Centicorns were half men and half horses, with a pointed bone spiraling from their forehead. They also had markings on their back thighs that they took great pride in. The problem was, the creatures were not fond of me after I borrowed and sold one of their precious gems.

As I inspected the hoof prints, I came across something that restored my faith. One particular set of tracks was sunk more deeply in the sand than the others! That could only mean one thing, Morby was riding one of them! He must had convinced the Centicorns to take him to find his family. Perhaps Slipshod landed everyone safely and Morby would be reunited with them, once again. What was in it for the Centicorns, I didn't know, but one thing was for sure- Morby had my magical dagger and I wasn't about to give up on getting it back!

I shook off the excess water and stretched my legs for a moment. Then, I took off in the direction of the tracks. With any luck, my Boots of Speeding would have me up to this group in no time flat!

Chapter 12

I followed the Centicorn tracks for a couple of miles. They led around the lake and headed straight into the desert. I didn't like the thought of following them out into the hot sand, but what choice did I have? Fortunately for me, I spotted a rising dust cloud in the sky, and that could mean only one thing: Slipshod had crashed!

It wasn't long before I could see the form of the fallen dragon taking shape in the distance. I decided to approach the scene, cautiously, so I slowed my pace and crept over to a nearby mesa. My Blending Cloak helped me stay out of sight, and my Ring of Spider

Climbing helped me get about 30 feet above the ground to a small area where I could get a better view.

From what I could tell, a good number of the passengers survived. It must have been a hard landing for poor Slipshod, though, because there was a long deep trench in the sand about a hundred feet long and smeared with his blood. I could not tell if he was alive, but I knew if he was, he probably wouldn't last long. The Centicorns would probably put the dying dragon out of its misery to make sure he wasn't a threat. After a few minutes of scanning the scene, I spotted big ol' Morby sitting on the ground surrounded by his wife and weird-looking kid. To my dismay, I also spotted Dunfer, who was shouting at him while holding my dagger!

The Centicorn's seemed to be helping Dunfer; perhaps they had taken Magurk from Morby and given it to him. I wondered if it was Dunfer's plan all along to hijack the dragon, take its passengers near Dociletoff, and then sell them off as slaves after robbing them. This evil practice had my blood boiling. I hated slave trading of any sort. My mind immediately thought of things to do with Dunfer when I got my dagger back. Plus, honestly, I was not too fond of the Centicorns either. The foul beasts unapologetically left droppings everywhere and acted like it didn't stink. As a teen working at MacGregors Tavern, I remember the way they would trot up to the ride through window, and I'd always mess with them.

They would say, "Hay!"

I'd say "Hey," twisting the spelling of the word to greet them back.

"No, you dolt," they'd reply. "I said haaay."

"I said hey back," I replied. "Don't be so rude."

I'd watch them get angrier and angrier the longer I kept the joke going.

Finally, they would shout, "Straw! Straw! We're hungry! We want straw!"

"Okay, okay," I'd reply before returning to the window with a handful of drinking straws.

They'd complain to Mr. MacGregor, and I'd be reprimanded, but it was always worth it. I enjoyed messing with the uppity creatures any chance I got. But today, out here in the desert, they wouldn't just complain about me; I had a nagging feeling they'd stomp me to death with their hooves.

At this distance, I could see that there was about eight Centicorns milling about holding spears and axes; which are their favored weapons. I counted roughly forty survivors, but most of them were ordinary people. It didn't look like there was any adventuring class among them. There was a dead elf at the largest Centicorn's feet, so I took it that he was probably the only one with enough bravery or stupidity to take on the creatures. It was at times like this that I appreciated having my lich eye. It helped me see farther than my normal human eye.

I wished my magical Swatfly bow could shoot that far, because I would have knocked off a couple of the creatures before they realized they were under attack. I sat down on a ledge and tried to develop a plan to rescue my precious dagger and the others. I wasn't too far into my thoughts when I heard some clanking not far from me and looked over. I couldn't believe my luck. Climbing down the rocks was Bok and Choy, the ninja archers that belonged to the adventuring party I traveled with the most. "We should wait for nightfall, Bok."

"I like to see what I'm shooting at," Bok replied. "Unlike you, and the mess you leave on the outhouse seat lid at 2 a.m.!"

"Just be glad he's a lot better aim with his bow," I said, startling them both.

They nearly fell off the cliff in shock before scrambling to grab their weapons. "Gwai Lo! You nearly gave us a heart attack!"

I laughed at them, and then slowly started to climb down alongside the twin brothers. "C'mon, you two," I said. "Let's go do some rescuing."

"I've got to get one of those rings," Bok said, watching me quickly scuttle down the cliff front.

"What are you two doing here?" I asked, watching them from the ground as they finished their descent. "Where are all the others?"

"We were on a side quest to acquire a rare magical item," Choy explained. "We left the others in Dociletoff. A chef at the De-jaView Tavern told us about it."

"I think I've eaten there before," I remarked, but Bok ignored me.

"She said it was located at the most famous oasis of the Bar-rendry desert. It's called the Ramseye Tavern, and it's hidden in some caves a few miles west of here. We talked to the owner, an ornery dwarf named Gordon, who we heard rumors of having possession of the item."

"Did he have it?" I asked.

"Yes, but he is not willing to part with it so easily," Bok said, smiling broadly.

"Gordon sent us on our way with a quest," Choy cut in. "If we can find something he desires to have, he is willing to trade."

"So, what is the item he requires?" I asked, not caring who answered.

"A dragon's brain!" both said back to me. "As fresh as possible."

"We walked out of the Ramseye feeling let down," Bok stated. "We couldn't imagine where in the realms we could find such a thing."

"That's when we heard something fly over our heads," Choy stated. "As Bok and I looked up, he was splashed with some blood from a dragon that was descending rather quickly! We couldn't believe our luck!"

"That's quite a coincidence," I stated, kind of amazed, myself.

"How did you get here, Gwai Lo?" Bok asked. "The last time we talked, you were on your way to the Palm Eye Finger Magic Shop in Neverspring to see Bub and Lar for some work. What happened?"

"It's a long story," I explained, "but it's not over yet."

The twins shrugged. They knew I didn't care to explain any further, so they let it go. Bok and Choy were good adventuring mates. They did their jobs, and they did them well. Both were deadly and quick with their weapons. They never backed down from a fight and were not afraid of anything, except maybe Aloonda, our pretty, blonde-haired magic-user. One of her steely-eyed glares let you know you were in trouble, especially after pulling one of their many pranks.

The two ninja archers were identical twins, but notably different from each other in many ways. Bok wore his hair long and was more impulsive and impatient. He was also kind of sloppy in appearance. His light leather armor was almost hidden by black clothing, which usually was stained or tattered. Although he used his short bow the most, he carried a small fruit knife that he lovingly named Gurnlik, which means brain lick in Gnomerian.

Choy, on the other hand, was neat and organized. He wore his hair short and kept a tidy appearance. The armor he wore was similar to his brother's, but properly worn and kept spotless. He was patient, sometimes too much so, if you ask me. He always seemed to be late for everything.

I watched Choy as he removed a scroll from his backpack. They both seemed excited about it for some reason. Bok unwound it to show me a drawing. "Yeah," I stated, "It's a frying pan, so what?"

"It's the magically enhanced item we're questing for," Choy stated. "Nothing ever sticks to it; it's easy to clean!"

I did appreciate that Choy was a fantastic cook and that he was excited about this new item, but I was a bit skeptical about its value as a real magical item. "I can fry four eggs and flip them, without ever touching a spatula!" he exclaimed.

"Speaking of spatulas," Bok said, rolling his eyes. "Show him what you did get."

Placing the scroll back, Choy then pulled out two long items, a ladle and a spatula. He spun these around in his hands and struck a fighting pose like they were deadly weapons. "I hope these are worth what we just paid," Bok stated. "Gordon from Ramseye was rude and insulting! I don't even want to go back for the pan."

"The Centicorns will be getting ready to march," I replied. "We better come up with a strategic maneuver soon, or both our plans will be nixed."

Bok looked at Choy for a moment, then they both looked at me and said, "Bait and slash!"

Ugh. I hated the bait and slash maneuver. It always meant that I was in the most danger.

Five minutes later, I was walking up to the group of Centicorns with my hands up. Bok and Choy were not far behind me, using my Blending Cloak to hide their presence. "Water," I pretended to croak out, "I need water."

The Centicorns let out a shout, but it was Dunfer who was the first to hobble forward. His leg was bandaged up from the dagger wound that Morby had given him. "Don't come any closer," he said, holding up my dagger. "You should have joined me when you had the chance, brother rogue. I'm going to make a fortune off the Centicorn slave trade; you could have been rich!"

"I'm not into horsing around," I calmly replied. "I take attainment of gold much more seriously."

I was only twenty or so feet away at this point and growing confident in our plan, but then the Centicorns started sniffing the air. "Something's wrong here," the largest one said, "I smell something!"

"It's a trap!" one of the other Centicorns shouted, as Bok and Choy let my cloak fall, revealing their bows.

Without hesitation, Dunfer let out a yell and flung Magurk at my face! Little did he know I'd been wielding this magical dagger for years, and I knew everything there was to know about how to handle it. I leaned back on one leg and grabbed it out of mid-air by the blade, and then flung it back at him full force! "Gurk..." was the last sound he muttered as my weapon split his unibrow in two!

Two of the Centicorns were dropped by heart shots from the two archers. At the same time, the others threw their spears at us. I ducked them and pulled out my bow, firing an arrow into the leg of the closest one. It howled out in pain and crumpled into the dirt. That's when four potential slave passengers jumped on it and started beating it with their bare hands!

Bok and Choy had dodged the projectiles thrown at them, as well. Then, they tried to pull out more arrows, but the Centicorns had gotten to them too fast and were now wielding their axes. I couldn't see what was happening after that, but I was almost at my dagger when I heard the battle cry of the leader of the Centicorns. He was just about to descend on me with his axe. Unfortunately for him, he did not notice the rotund human coming at him, tackling him from the side! It was Morby! "Get off my back," the leader neighed, "You're too heavy!"

With this pause, I pulled out another arrow and fired it at the large creature, hitting it in the belly. "Stay on!" I yelled out to Morby. "Don't let go!"

"I'm on him like glue!" the overweight man yelled back. "But hurry up, he's unstable!"

The Centicorn tried bucking Morby, but he was too wounded, and his rider was just too fat to throw off. So, with a quick motion, I pulled Magurk from Dunfer's forehead, did a roll, and then jammed the dagger right into the chest of the massive Centicorn! It went down quickly, crashing face-first, its final exhale sending out a small swirl of sand. When I looked around, I saw many newly freed passengers killing another Centicorn, and then I looked over at Bok and Choy. Bok's leather chest armor had been slashed open, and he was bleeding, but that did not stop him from repeatedly stabbing his opponent with Gurnlik, his trusty fruit knife! Next to him, Choy was beating another Centicorn with his magically-enhanced oversize spoon and spatula. The Centicorn couldn't move fast enough to block the ninja's weird cooking fight moves. Within moments, it was on the ground, unconscious.

The passengers let out a cheer as the remaining Centicorn's hot-hoofed it out of there, giving up on their plans. I let out a sigh and fell to my knees; I almost kissed the blade of Magurk, but decided not to because Dunfer's blood and eyebrow hairs were all over it. I couldn't help but smile, though; it felt good to have it back in my hand!

Morby walked over to me and slapped me on the back. "Thank you, rogue. I'll never forget what you and your two friends have done for my family and the other passengers."

"Well," I said, still catching my breath, "I do like gold."

The obese man laughed out loud and shook his head. "I figured that!"

He looked around for a minute and spotted the ring on Dunfer's hand. He walked over and knelt, slipping the ring off. Then, he stood up and starting walking over. Morby didn't notice Dunfer's split unibrow disappear, but I did. So, when he offered the ring to me as a gift, I quickly declined, sensing something was awry. "Your thanks is enough," I stated, nearly stumbling over the words I didn't think I'd ever hear myself say. "You keep it. You're a hero, too."

Morby smiled and slipped the ring on, which magically grew larger to fit his chubby finger. Then, a thick section of hair grew between his eyebrows, giving him a thick unibrow. He had no idea what had happened and turned around to show his wife, who noticed his new look and nearly swooned with joy! Now I knew he was super rich! Later on, I found out that the ring was called the Last Unibrow. Bub and Lar created it from the Palm Eye Finger Magic Shop as a prank. Once on, only a powerful magic spell or death could ever remove it.

The survivors slowly gathered their gear and decided to head to Dociletoff to look for a caravan to take them to Neverspring. The stewardess gave me a hug and a wink, then thanked the three of us for rescuing them from the Centicorns. "You must be a highly regarded hero," she said to me.

"That's me," I stated, while Bok and Choy chuckled. "I am sought by many."

Morby promised us a reward the next time we stopped by his office in Neverspring. "My family owes you a debt."

We waved goodbye after letting them know that we had a mission to complete. When all the people left, we walked over to Slipshod's corpse and tapped on his head. "How in the realms are we supposed to get his brain out of there?" I asked the two brothers. "I can't spend a week here; I need to get to Neverspring."

The three of us worked on it for over twenty minutes, cutting, slashing, and even jumping up and down on it. It was no use, and all that happened was that we could hear a squishing sound. "Do you hear that?" Choy said, "That's the sound of opportunity!"

"Listen, brother," Bok stated. "We're never going to get the brain out; the skull is too thick!"

"You boys need help?" a familiar booming voice shouted out from below us on the ground.

"Speaking of thick skulls," Bok laughed as we spotted YaMacha Derschingler, our party's barbarian holding up his giant magical war axe with his right arm.

"It might be a split decision," Choy chimed in, "but, yeah, we could use that axe of yours!"

Standing with YaMacha was the rest of my main traveling party: Aloonda the elven mage, Healy the Cleric, and Fodderman the Zombie. "You look a bit worse for wear," Healy said, climbing up with the rest of the group. "Need a quick pick me up?"

"Gladly," I said, "Do your magic!"

Healy laughed and cast some healing spells on us. It was such a relief; all my aches and pains were gone! Bok and Choy were pleased, as well. Then, they explained why we were upon the head of the dead dragon. Bok asked, "What made you leave Dociletoff to come out here?"

"Are you kidding?" Aloonda asked. "You could hear this dragon crashing for miles! We figured you two might be caught up in this mess, since you had said you were going to the Ramseye Tavern. But, for some reason, I'm not shocked to find our rogue tied up in this!"

"Trouble finds me," I explained. "Then, I stab it."

"Fodderman! Quit biting the dragon!" Healy said, shooing the zombie trying to bite through the dragon's hide to get to its brain.

"So if you help us get this out of the skull," Bok stated. "We can trade it for a magical frying pan!"

YaMacha looked intrigued. "Does this mean you'll cook more?"

"Sure," Choy replied. "Lot's more!"

"Stand back," YaMacha stated, spitting into his hands before picking up his large axe. "This requires a delicate touch!"

It only took YaMacha five minutes to chop around the skull, revealing the twin brother's prize. "He didn't give that brain a second thought," I whispered to Aloonda, who chuckled at my joke.

Thanks to YaMacha's amazing strength and Healy's ingenuity,

we were soon dragging the brain on a couple of sewn together blankets across the Barrendry desert. "This brain pan better be worth it," YaMacha complained as we drug the object toward the Ramseye Tavern.

It took the whole crew to drag the disgusting and smelly thing along. Except for Aloonda, that is, her job was to keep Fodderman back from it using a leash that Healy had made for special occasions such as this. "He's starving," she complained. "Can't we just give him a nibble?"

"No way," Choy refused. "It's all or nothing with this deal!"

Chapter 13

We arrived at the Ramseye just as the sun set. Patrons from the tavern came out and marveled at the giant brain, now illuminated by torchlight. "Well, I'll be an orc's donkey," Gordon said, stepping out of the front door before whistling. "You did it!"

"That's right," Choy panted. "I'm here for the magic pan."

Gordon's eyebrows went up, and he rubbed his graying dwarfish beard before circling the brain, inspecting it closely. "Tsk, tsk," he began. "This is a green dragon's brain, isn't it?"

"Yeah," Bok said. "So, what?"

"Well, you see, I was kind of thinking of a red dragon," he stated. "Maybe I could offer you a magic skillet, instead?"

"That wasn't the deal," Choy said, marching over to look down at the dwarf. "You never said what color dragon!"

"That's my offer," the dwarf said with a grin. "Take it or leave it!"

"Let's make a new deal," Choy stated, pulling out his bow and aiming it at Gordon's nose. "I want that pan, just like in the original deal!"

"Put the bow down," came a voice from the small crowd now gathered outside. "Or you won't leave here with anything at all!"

A well-armored gnoll fighter appeared behind Choy and held the point of his sword in his back. A wizard stood beside him, and his hands began to glow as he mumbled his words. Choy laughed.

"Is this your crew? I think you'll need a small army, not these two clowns."

The rest of the crowd pulled out daggers, swords, and even a few dinner forks. Gordon grinned, "This is my small army!"

"And this is Choy's," YaMacha stated, lifting his glowing blue axe and standing at full height. "I've been looking forward to splitting more skulls!"

Bok had his bow out, Healy was chanting, Aloonda's hands immediately started flaming, and I held up Magurk before vanishing right before their eyes with my Cloak of Blending. Fodderman was now loose, and he wasted no time diving at the dragon brain and gobbling big chunks from it!

It was only silent for five seconds, but it seemed a lot longer. "It was only a joke!" Gordon sputtered out, nervously. "Queeznarf, Wolfgag, lower your weapons. It was only me making a funny!"

We all knew it wasn't a joke, but everyone lowered their weapons. "Of course, you can have Tufflon, my magic non-stick frying pan," Gordon said in a defeated tone. "A deal is a deal, after all. Oh, and can you call off your zombie?"

After Gordon and his crew hauled the brain into his kitchen, we found a dark corner of the tavern to relax in. I think we were all starving by this point. The dwarf promised everyone that the food we were about to eat would blow our minds. The place was at capacity, and everyone was excited to see what kind of meal the dwarf would be making with the giant brain. Except for Fodderman, that is, he was looking full, already. I don't know if you've ever smelled a burp from a zombie with a green dragon's brain on its breath, but I can tell you it's quite awful.

After a while, the kitchen doors flew open, and the crowd cheered as the Ramseye waitstaff wheeled out tray after tray of oddly delicious smelling food. Healy and I had ordered the dragon brain stew, while YaMacha got his portion pan-seared with some spicy dipping sauce. Bok, Choy, and Aloonda got theirs baked in a marmalade sauce with sticks of cinnamon. Aloonda stuck one of her sticks into Fodderman's mouth. "You're never going to meet a nice zombie girl with breath like that!" she said.

To our surprise, the food was probably the best we'd ever had. It was no wonder Gordon of the Ramseye, was considered one of the realm's top chefs. Everyone ate in silence, savoring every bite. Choy ate his food happily while holding Tufflon, his new frying pan, in his lap. "With this pan, I can be just as good a chef as Gordon," he claimed. "I wonder what other culinary magic items he uses."

The others muttered in agreement and nodded but kept chewing. I, on the other hand, wondered about that, too. I gently pushed my empty bowl away and looked toward the kitchen, pondering.

"Nature calls," I said, standing up. "I'll be back in a minute."

As I walked toward the restrooms, I could see Gordon and his staff joyfully talking with other patrons. I gave him a thumbs up when he looked my way. He seemed pleased. After closing the restroom door behind me, I checked to see if I was alone and activated my Cloak of Blending. Then, I waited a few moments until another patron came in. Then, I ran around him and through the door before it shut again. I crept along the wall and made my way to the kitchen, and then slipped in when one of the waitstaff came out.

I scanned the kitchen for anything unusual. My lich eye picked up a magical glow from some small utensils, so I grabbed them and put them into my magical Sack of Holding. I spotted another door in the back of the kitchen and quickly made my way to it. It was locked. Not for long, though. I was surprised that a dwarf like Gordon didn't have a much better security system installed.

Inside, I found tables covered with spice ingredients, scrolls with recipes, and to my surprise, an endless supply of paperclips. The paperclips were bent in an assorted variety of angles, and there were scattered notes all around. It seems the dwarf was obsessed with trying to reinvent the paperclip. His writings were mostly math equations and sketches that focused on the little pieces of bendable metal. The words were dwarven with lots of exclamation points behind them, so I had no idea what they said. "He's eccentric, but man, can he cook," I mumbled as I looked around for stuff to steal.

I hurriedly gathered up a lot of the spice ingredients; I figured Aloonda might be able to use them, and then checked around for secret doors. That's when I heard the doorknob to the room turn. I quietly slid by a cabinet. I watched Gordon enter the room with a small utensil in his hand, and from the way it glowed magically, I knew it was something I wanted. The dwarf walked up to a small painting of two carrots dancing on a beach and moved it out of the way, revealing a hidden safe.

Gordon kissed the item, then whispered, "My lucky melon baller, you've done it again!"

The dwarf placed the item in the safe with some other stuff and closed it before turning the combination lock. He put the painting back and ran his finger over the frame, whispering, "Soon."

After he turned around and left the room, I waited a moment. When the coast was clear, I sprinted over and removed the amusing piece of art off the wall and stuck it into my bag. Who knew, maybe this gaudily painted piece of slapdashery could net me a few coins at Fancyplants Art Gallery. I was certain that Baghurl the Elf would be interested in acquiring it. I grinned as I focused on the safe, moving the dial on the combination with the same numbers I watched him move. Then, voila! Everything was quickly transferred into my Sack of Holding.

I silently crept back out and joined my group after becoming visible again in the restroom. "What took you so long?" Aloonda asked.

"Too much brain food," I said, patting my belly. "I just had to clear some thoughts."

YaMacha found this highly amusing and pounded on the table with his fist as he erupted in laughter. "They better hope I don't have to clear mine," he guffawed. "I'll clear the whole room!"

Everyone laughed, and Gordon came over to check on us. "How was the meal?" he asked.

"I've never had a dragon's brain before," I replied. "All of a sudden, I feel enriched."

"Excellent," the dwarf said happily. "I'm glad everything worked out between us! Would your party like to stay for dessert?"

"We need to go," I said, standing up. "I have some business I need to attend to."

"Bah!" YaMacha growled. "There's always room for dessert!"

"Yeah," Choy chimed in, "Let's see what else is on the menu!"

I gave the archer a hard stare and raised an eyebrow, "Ixnay on the essertday," I whispered loudly.

YaMacha gave me a grimace. The rest of the party followed suit. They knew I had pulled something. "Um, yes," Healy chimed in. "We really must be going; we're up past our bedtime."

Gordon frowned. "Bedtime? What is going on here? I thought you were mighty warriors of the realms!"

"Mighty warriors need sleep," YaMacha stated, placing his hand on the handle of his axe. "Or we get cranky!"

It wasn't long before we were out in the cool night air and marching through the sand, heading west toward Neverspring. The giant barbarian grumbled the whole way. "Instead of dessert, I get the desert. This switch does not make me happy, rogue!"

"When you guys see what I got, you'll be more than happy," I replied. "I promise."

We all gathered around some rocks that were near the edge of the mountain range and Aloonda cast a light spell. Everyone surrounded me as I pulled the first item out of the bag. The first thing was the melon baller. "This is a magic eye gouger," I told YaMacha. "It's for you."

"Yes!" he shouted, holding it up in the air. "I will name it, Eyesore, after what it leaves my enemies!"

"Aloonda, I got you some spell components," I said, handing her a few fistfuls. "I hope they are handy!"

She gasped. "Spider tongue, Werespud, Scarfenmauw, Tween-tow Moss, Snowgrass, and Dooperwart! These are fantastic!"

"What did I get?" Choy asked.

I reached into the Sack of Holding and pulled out a handful of scrolls. "Original recipes from Ramseye Gordon! Wow!"

"I can't wait to see mine," Bok said, stepping forward.

After I placed a potato peeler in his hand, he gave me a look of disappointment. "A potato peeler? Are you kidding me?"

"It's a magic potato peeler," I explained. "You can peel potatoes twice as fast!"

"Hmph," Bok grumbled, walking away ungrateful.

"This is for you, Healy," I said, tossing him a spice bottle. "All it says on it is Healthful Hurbz."

The cleric twisted off the cap and smelled it. "Mmm. It smells good. It's definitely got some healing magic in it."

I pulled two more spices out of my bag. "Check these out," I stated. "One says Campfire Kick, and the other just says Secret."

YaMacha came over and smelled both of them. "I want this one," he said, grabbing the Campfire Kick. "It gets my blood pumping!"

I shrugged and put the one labeled Secret back into my Sack of Holding. I didn't know what it tasted like or did, but Bub and Lar would probably be able to let me know sooner or later. "We better get moving," I said to the rest of my party. "This cool night air is the only thing that will help us as we travel to Neverspring. We have to make it at least to the Dragondrop Mall before the sun comes up."

"I don't think Gordon is going to be happy when he sees a bunch of his stuff missing, either," Choy added. "Bok and I will stay to the rear, watching for any activity behind us."

"Good," YaMacha stated. "Gwai Lo, run ahead and scout. We won't be far behind."

"Sure thing," I replied. "Piece of cake."

As I ran ahead, I could hear YaMacha immediately begin ranting about the dessert he missed. He didn't sound happy, so I was glad to put as much distance between us as possible.

Chapter 14
After a half-hour of scouting ahead, I thought I heard a horse

neighing to the south. I cautiously ran in that direction and spotted something I thought would be helpful; a small caravan. I knew that these travelers might not want to have company. After all, the Unremembered Realms is a dangerous place. I had to find out, though, because the thought of walking the rest of the way to Neverspring made me more tired than I already was. Plus, the idea of Gordon of the Ramseye discovering his missing goods might not go too well for us. We had to put more distance between the Dwarf's small army and my party. I ran back to my team and let them know what I discovered.

I led them to a place where I thought the slow-moving caravan would cross, and we set our ingenious plan into motion. Aloonda always hated this, but she was a pretty blonde and has gotten more whoops and whistles than a shuffleball game. "Fine," she grumbled, agreeing reluctantly, "but I swear this is the last time!"

We all knew it wouldn't be, but we compassionately nodded while holding back our smiles. A few moments later, the wizardess was standing by where the wagons were going to pass. She stuck her thumb out and flashed a great big smile. When the lead wagon spotted Aloonda, they pulled up next to her. "Would you fellas mind helping an elf gal out? I could sure use a lift."

She batted her eyelashes, and the two human males driving the wagon swooned. "Gosh, lady," the brown-haired one began. "What's a purty gal like you doin' out here? Y'all ain't some kinda shapeshifter, are ya?"

The heavier, dark-haired one hit him with his hat. "Where're your manners, Rooben. Can't you see this is a damsel in distress? Don't be so rude."

"Sorry, Bascotty," Rooben responded. "My apologies, ma'am. It's just that we got to git our goods to the Dragondrop Mall by sunrise. It would be hard getting' em' there if we's both dead."

"What's the hold-up?!" came a shout from one of the two wagons behind the first one.

"Be quiet, you crusty old goat!" Bascotty shouted back. "We'll be off in a second!"

"So you don't mind helping me out?" Aloonda asked.

"Not at all," Rooben answered. "As a matter of fact, you can ride in our wagon with us!"

"Such gentlemen," she smiled before turning around and placing two fingers in her mouth to let out a whistle. "C'mon, boys!"

I always enjoyed the looks on their faces when my party came out from where they were hiding. Today, it happened to be a large gathering of rocks. "But, but…" was all either of them could mutter.

Both men knew better than to push it any further when YaMacha came into view. "Don't worry," he began. "We just need a ride, and from the looks of it, you could use a little security."

These words helped Rooben and Bascotty calm down and not be so flustered. Aloonda climbed up between the two men, which made them even happier, while YaMacha climbed in the back. Bok and Choy went to the rear wagon while Healy, Fodderman, and I climbed into the middle. "You boys comfy?" The older man driving the wagon asked.

We nodded up to him after we sat in the back with a bunch of filled sacks. "What's in these?" Healy asked, "Gold?"

"I don't think so," I said. "I'd be able to smell it."

"Those are all buttons," the old man laughed as he snapped the reins, getting the horses to move. "There's a store in the Dragondrop Mall called Stitch That. Our village, Wovenspun, is just northwest of Turridsville. We're the shop's main button supplier."

"I've heard of your village," Healy stated. "They've really gotten it together in the last couple of years."

"Sounds exciting," I yawned.

The older man harumphed. "Don't think there aren't dangers, rogue," he explained. "Turridsville is always raiding us for our buttons. Their leader is an awful Garbarian, named…"

"Jordash," I said, completing his sentence. "Trust me; I know your plight. There's nothing worse when a barbarian forces his way into the fashion industry. I barely got out of a predicament there, myself."

"Durley," Healy said, reading the name written on one of the sacks. "That's your name?"

"Yes, sir," he said proudly. "Durley of Durley's Buttons. We'll have you together in a cinch!"

Healy and the old coot got into a long conversation about the history of buttons, so I took the chance to doze out. The last thing I remember before falling asleep was seeing Fodderman chewing on Grody, his orc gut teddy bear. I hadn't been asleep for more than a couple of hours when I woke up to Healy tapping my shoulder. "Hey, Gwai Lo," he said. "Wake up."

"Are we there yet?" I said groggily, noticing it was still dark.

"No," the cleric answered. "But I'm hungry, and I was wondering what kind of rations you have."

"Just some of the dried dragon brain meat I saved from my plate," I said, rubbing my eyes. "What do you have?"

"That's great," Healy stated. "Because I have some bread. We could divvy up what we have and make some…"

"Sand Witches!" Durley shouted from the front of the wagon. "We're being ambushed by Sand Witches!"

"There's enough for three," Healy said. "But I wouldn't call it an ambush."

"No, not sandwiches," Durley yelled. "I mean, five Sand Witches are blocking our path, and they are attacking the caravan!"

I had heard of Sand Witches before. They lived inside caves and fed off any adventurers who they could find wandering through the desert. They preyed mostly on the weak and weary, so they were in for a surprise on this night! Healy and I stuck our heads out front from underneath the wagon's covering and saw the ugly hags floating about six feet off the ground, riding sand whirlwinds. They were waving their hands around and chanting something in unison. Within seconds, a fifteen-foot-high sand golem rose from the desert and rammed its fists into the third wagon, smashing it to pieces! Bok and Choy had leaped from it only seconds before, but the two buttoneers driving flew to the ground in crumpled heaps! Thousands of buttons flew into the air and fell like colorful snow.

The witches all let out a cackle, but it didn't last long, because Aloonda stood up and shouted, "Is that all you got?!"

With a few motions and mumbles of her own, she cast a spell. All the spilled buttons, and ones from the other wagons' bags, came together to form a golem of their own. The button golem immediately tackled the sand golem and was punching it with its multi-colored fists! "A button golem?!" YaMacha hollered above the din to Aloonda. "That, I wasn't expecting!"

The button golem was much smaller than the sand one, but it was distracting enough for it to let us have a go at the witches who had us in a pickle. "I'm full of surprises," Aloonda laughed as the barbarian leaped from the wagon.

YaMacha gripped his magical axe and ran straight at the perplexed Sand Witches, who he planned on slicing in half. By the time Healy, Fodderman, and I got out of our wagon, the witches had spread out and had begun casting new spells. I pulled out my Swatfly bow and fired at one of them, but she dodged the arrow almost effortlessly. The Sand Witch wasn't able to escape the lightning bolt which came down from the sky, though! Healy's spell electrified her, causing her to scream out in pain before her sandy whirlwind disappeared and she fell to the ground. Her yellow eyes creeped me out as I ran up with Magurk and tried finishing the job. She scratched me with her claw-like nails across my face and then threw me off with extraordinary strength!

That did not stop me, though, because I just tumbled through sand and buttons when I landed and quickly jumped back on my feet. The Sand Witch leaped up and would have taken a bite out of me, but I thrust Magurk into the air, and I felt it breaking through her rib cage! She fell to the ground without further sound. The Sand Golem howled out in pain and shrunk in size as the witch died. "Kill the witches," Bok shouted while dodging a blow from the sand creature. The animated monster pushed the button golem over to take a swing at him. "It's weakening the Sand Golem!"

YaMacha had almost reached the witches when they hit him with a Sand Blast spell, throwing him backward. Such a powerful blast would have crushed a normal man, but YaMacha just stood back up, shaking sand from his hair. He was smiling and I think that unnerved the Sand Witches. "You crusty old hags," he laughed.

"I'm not some poor boy you found sizzling in the desert!"

He threw his magical axe at full force and cleaved one of the witches completely in half! Again, the Sand Golem groaned and shrunk in size. By this time, Choy was whacking it with his new pan, Tufflon, while Bok was running up to help us. The remaining three Sand Witches separated and started blasting us with all sorts of sand spells. One cast a Quicken Sand below my feet, and I began to sink. If Healy hadn't grabbed my arm, I would have been consumed by the desert! The other cast a Swirly Spell that picked Aloonda, Rooben, and Bascotty up from the wagon and spun them around in the air. The third tried to cast something at YaMacha, but he had grabbed Fodderman and hurled the zombie at her. "You're toast, Sand Witch!" he yelled.

She screamed and fell to the ground as Fodderman hit her at full force! She scratched and clawed at Fodderman while he tore into her. She had clawed his face and bitten his ear off, but that didn't bother the undead hero. The Sand Witch was just a midnight snack to him. The Sand Golem wailed again as it shrunk, and the Button Golem was now getting the better of him. Clumps of sand were falling off him as the remaining two witches' magic was too weak to maintain it. Fearing for their lives, they grabbed the third wagon's drivers' bodies and fled off into the desert on twirling twisters of sand.

"Taboon! Cherbadda!" Durley yelled after them. "No!"

"Forget about them, Durley!" Rooben groaned from the ground where he had fallen after the Swirly spell wore off. "They knew the risk when getting into the button business!"

Durley looked off into the distance, then nodded. "You're right, Rooben. We have got to get this shipment of buttons to the Dragondrop mall by opening time. It's what they would have wanted. Thanks for the help, strangers. You saved the day."

"It's just another normal day for us," YaMacha said, wiping globs of blood from his axe. "I have worked up an appetite, though. Does anyone have an actual sandwich?"

We decided to leave the smashed wagon and take the two horses that pulled it. I opted to ride one, because Fodderman reeked of Sand Witch innards. Aloonda mounted the other one after she ordered the Button Golem to float itself back into the sacks from which it came. She then used another spell to handily levitate the remaining buttons scattered around and floated them into bags, as well. "That's handy," Durley stated, watching the magic. The rest of the party loaded into the remaining two wagons, and we managed to make it through the desert the rest of the night with no other incidents. As the sun started to rise, we caught the silhouette of the hardened stone dragon, which made up the Dragondrop Mall.

For those not familiar with this part of the Unremembered Realms, the Dragondrop Mall was created when an ancient red dragon of legendary size fell in love with a medusa. After it was accidentally turned to stone, desert gnomes carved out its insides and created a beautiful place for shoppers to come to buy goods. The medusa had enslaved the gnomes for many years, that is until I had come along. I managed to find the snake-haired creatures secret lair and dispatch her with Magurk. The gnomes have been grateful to me ever since. Many shopkeepers had no idea what transpired with the medusa; they only knew that the gnomes seemed much more at peace.

When our group got closer, the buttoneers told us we had to wait for the doors to open and for them to clear out the Mallwalkers. Apparently, all the other suppliers knew about this, too, because dozens of wagons were parked outside, just like us. "What are Mallwalkers?" Bok asked Durley.

"For some reason, the mall attracts zombies," Durley began while pointing to the doors.

The old man was right. Dozens of undead scratched at the windows, trying to get in so they could eat the brains of shoppers. "Usually, they show up during the night," Durley continued. "Legend has it that there was a battle in the desert a few hundred years ago when an evil cleric had opened a portal to the plane of the dead and started bringing in zombies to help his takeover. The only thing that stopped him was an elven archer named Bonearrow. He slayed the cleric in an epic battle and thought he had sealed the doorway to the plane of the dead. Unfortunately, there is still a small crack that lets a few zombies through, now and again."

"Nobody has ever found this crack?" YaMacha asked.

"Not that we know of," Bascotty replied. "But I could only imagine the reward for the heroes who could find it and shut it down."

YaMacha smiled, leaned back in his seat, and muttered, "Hmmm...."

Durley pointed to the row of glass doors of the entrance that led into the mall. "Look, they've sent out the morning cleric."

A tired-looking cleric, holding a coffee cup, walked up to the doors. He yawned, then took a drink of coffee while the zombies scratched at the glass, trying to get to him. The cleric calmly set his cup down, reached into a side pouch, and pulled out a symbol of turning. Then, he tapped on it and held it up. Some of the undead turned to dust while stronger ones fled. Healy held a hand over Fodderman's eyes as the zombie leaned out of the wagon to hear what the other zombie cries were about. "Let's drop off these buttons," Durley said, hopping down from the wagon.

When I looked over, I could see the cleric unlocking the doors and waving for all the vendors to come in. Other people started unloading and carrying their supplies into the mall. I grabbed a couple of reasonably sized stacks of buttons and started walking inside. "I'll be along in a minute," Healy stated. "I've got to disguise Fodderman, so he doesn't get turned to dust."

I didn't know what Healy's plans were, but he was resourceful, and I knew he'd come up with something. As I strolled in, I noticed the location placard, and I stopped to look for where the Stitch That shop was located. "Where is the store at, Gwai Lo?" Aloonda asked as she walked up behind me. "I hope it's close. These bags are heavy."

"The second floor," I said, pointing on the map. "Just up the magic stairwell and about six shops down to the right.

After letting the stairs escalate us up to the top floor, we dropped the bags off. Stitch That's owner, a friendly female gnome named Louise Buhtton greeted us, happily. After everyone dropped off the rest of the sacks, we said goodbye to the buttoneers, and even accepted a bit of gold from them as a thank you. "Nice disguise," I said to Healy, looking at how he had dressed Fodderman.

The zombie had a long blonde wig that covered most of his face, a full flower print dress, and a wide-brimmed straw hat. He looked absolutely ridiculous. "It was the best I could do," Healy replied. "It's not like they have a disguise shop here, you know."

"Actually, it's in section L3," I replied, laughing. "Didn't you read the placard?"

Healy frowned. "Well, that's just great," he said. "What a waste of gold."

"Maybe Aloonda will like it," I commented, turning to the mage.

"It's pretty," she stated. "But I'm not wearing it after Fodderman. Zombie stank never washes out."

YaMacha was pacing back and forth. "Is everyone ready to go yet? I want to search for the opening to the plane of death. I want to claim whatever reward there is for destroying it."

"Not until I'm done shopping," Aloonda said. "We're at the Dragondrop Mall, and I've got some gold. Sorry big guy, but this girl is picking up some accessories!"

"But, but," the barbarian stuttered.

"I'll start with some handbags," Aloonda said. "Here, 'macha, hold my old one!"

YaMacha was a giant mauler who would face an army of orcs, undead, or even giants by himself, but there was no way he was going to win against Aloonda right now. Healy and I grinned at his feeble attempts to wriggle out of it. "But think of adventure," he began. "Wouldn't you feel better knowing that you've stopped hordes of undead?! Come on, woman!"

"Alright," she replied, looking up at him. "If you feel so strongly about that, let's talk about those feelings."

"I, uh, you see, umm…" YaMacha stammered, getting all flustered.

"Listen," she continued. "There's a BOGO sale at Bootlocker. I saw the sign on the way in here, and I'm not missing out!"

YaMacha hung his head, turned around, and started walking out. "I'm going to Food Court," he grumbled.

"Don't go too far," she yelled after him. "I'll need some money, and then your opinion on blouses!"

The barbarian groaned and continued off as Healy and I chuckled. "Well," I said. "If we're going to be awhile, I'm going to head over to the poison store."

The Poison Well was my favorite shop in the mall. It was owned by Roger Mortis, or Rigormorty, as I called him. The place had every option you could think of, and he always had the latest and greatest poisons on the market. Any rogue with half a brain shopped at Roger's place, so he was always making a killing. When he saw me walk in, he had a great big grin, "Welcome back, ghost man," he cheerfully stated. "Pick your poison!"

We shot the breeze for a bit on local scuttlebutt before he pulled out a case from below the counter. "I've been saving this just for you," he began. "It hasn't officially come out on the market yet. But I figured that since you're my top customer, I'd let you get your claw on it first."

He opened the box and pulled out a gorgeous red vial labeled "Brain Death." The dark liquid swirled inside and almost seemed to crawl up the glass imprisoning it. "One drop of this can melt a humanoid brain in less than five minutes," he proudly proclaimed. "It'll even kill the undead!"

"Whoa," I replied in awe. "That's so cool! Aggression is going to be so jealous!"

I could picture an orc captain, sitting down at his meal and halfway through, shouting "Brain melt!" before collapsing face-first into his porridge while I steal his belongings. I could also picture the look on some dopey ogre's face when his brain bursts like a pimple from his ears... that's when I quit daydreaming and reached into my pocket for gold to pay Rigormorty. When I pulled my hand out to count coins, which I have plenty of, there was one missing... my Coin of Cheating! In its place was an equally sized blue button.

"Are you okay?" Rigormorty asked. "You've suddenly gone pale!"

I quickly thought back to what must have happened. It must have fallen out in the battle with the Sand Witches. The blue button must have gotten into my pocket during the whirlwind of buttons when Aloonda cast that spell, which made them come from all around us and go back into the sacks. I bet my coin was still with them! I had to get back to Louise Buhtton's, quickly! "Hold that for me!" I shouted back to Rigormorty as I ran out the door.

The Dragondrop Mall was packed, so I had to dodge quite a few people on my way back to Stitch That! When I got there, Louise was organizing buttons into bins and singing to herself. "Louise," I huffed, trying to catch my breath. "I need to go through the buttons. I lost something!"

"Sure," she nodded. "Was it anything in particular?"

"A gold coin," I explained. "It was a lucky gold coin."

"Oh," she said. "Today is your lucky day. Here, I found three of them."

I was elated for a moment as she pulled them from her pocket and handed them to me. But the feeling left when I could see none of them were my precious Coin of Cheating. "None of these are it," I said. "You didn't find any more?"

"No," she stated. "But I haven't been through all of them, yet; I was too busy helping customers."

"Do you mind if I help sort through the buttons?" I asked. "Maybe I can find it."

"If you help sort them into their proper bins and don't leave a mess," Louise replied. "Go ahead."

When she left to help her customers, I began to sort but got impatient quickly. I started grabbing handfuls of buttons and chucked them into any closest bin. I found a few more of my gold coins, but after a half-hour of searching, I came to the bottom of the last bag. "I can't find my missing coin!" I said in a raised voice, above the din of customers. "Are you sure this is everything?"

Louise, looking upset, left a customer and came over. "Listen, I'm sorry you can't find your coin, but I've got customers and … wait a minute," she thoughtfully drifted off for a moment. "I did have a customer in here a little while ago who was looking for a gift for his girlfriend. But then only bought a small bag of buttons. I thought that was weird, but he sure was happy about it."

My heart sank. "What did this customer look like?" I asked. "Maybe I can find him."

"Oh, that's easy," she replied. "He's a halfling fellow. Quite handsome."

"There could be a hundred halflings shopping here today," I stated. "How do I know which one?"

"Well," Louise responded. "He's got a backpack full of treasure maps. He tried trading one for the bag of buttons."

"Robbie!" I said, clenching my fist in front of me.

"Oh, you know him?" was the last words I heard from Louise as I ran from the store.

I knew Robbie the Thief all right, and today was not going to be as lucky for him as he thought. Angrily, I stormed back over to the Poison Well for the Brain Melt. If everything worked out, Robbie wouldn't be so happy about his lucky find, but I do believe he was soon going to be going out of his mind!

Chapter 15

The mall was a big place and there were hundreds of humanoids of all types roaming from shop-to-shop, browsing, or purchasing things. Normally, I'd be spending most of my day picking some pockets or shoplifting something nice for my girlfriend, Amberfawn. Instead, here I was tracking down Robbie the Thief and fantasizing about choking the snot of him.

I casually peeked into many shops. First, there was Fencers, which had a lot of novelties. Then, I checked out Aberzombie & Ditch, which specialized in clothing that had been worn by the living dead. Judging from the pimple-faced teens I saw wearing their clothes, they reminded me of just that!

I tried Famous Bootwear, Build-a-Bugbear, the angry barbarian shop called Rantz (which I hear is all the rage), Bath and Body

Smithery, and even Things Unremembered.

I was starting to lose hope, and that's when I saw Healy standing in line at Gockies, the mall's famous cookie shop. "Have you seen Robbie the Thief come by here?"

"You bet I did," he said. "I just came out of Hot Subject and spotted him trying to flirt with Fodderman by the doorway. He really thought our zombie was a woman!"

Fodderman gurgled, and some drool spilled from his rotting lips. "This costume is working better than I thought!" He proudly proclaimed while straightening out Fodderman's wig.

"Where is he now?" I asked impatiently.

"I saw him go into Fadz," he replied. "You know, the store where they sell all the latest trends in clothing."

"You mean the one run by garbarians?" I replied. "No wonder everyone is dressing so terrible nowadays."

"Terribly trendy, I suppose," Healy was saying as I ran off.

"I've got to catch the little slime," I yelled back. "I'll catch up with you later!"

I maneuvered my way around some people and made it to the Fadz store, only to see a large number of people going in and coming out. I was thinking of entering, but then I heard a deep voice yell out, "Stop! Thief!"

Robbie ran out of the shop and hit me head-on, knocking me down. He dropped a small sack, and coins spill out in every direction! Patrons and some kids hollered with delight and started picking up all the coins. "You idiot!" Robbie and I shouted at each other simultaneously. "Watch where you're going!"

We made eye contact for a split second before both spitting out the words, "My coin!"

The large garbarian shop owner ran out of his shop and yelled, "There you are, you thieving weasel!"

I assumed he was talking to me, but he ran toward Robbie. In a panic, Robbie jumped up and tried to run, but my foot must have accidentally got in the way, and he tripped, falling flat on his face. "Thanks, buddy," the awfully dressed garbarian said while picking the halfling up.

Robbie, dangling five feet off the floor, wiped the blood from his nose and hissed, "I'll find you, Gwai Lo. Then, I'll take my dagger and... urk!"

The owner of Fadz began strangling the little oaf. I'd have stuck around to laugh or offer a helping hand, but I needed to rescue my coin. I scanned the area where the coins flew and noticed that most of them were gone. I concentrated with my lich eye, and a small blue flicker of light shining caught my attention. It was in the hand of a little female gnome who was getting ready to throw it into the mall's large fountain. I don't understand why people do this. Everyone knows wish fountains are all make-believe. If you want a wish granted, you need to find a magic ring or a djinn, and even then, the wish will probably be cursed, somehow. The outcome was usually determined by the DM, which is short for djinn's mood. The last time I tried a wish, I was nearly strangled to death by a small octopus.

As I hurried over to the gnome, I realized who it was. "Nissa Nackle Nim!" I stated cheerfully. "Allo, allo, you old bird!"

Nissa flipped the coin into the fountain, then turned around, looking up at me. "Why, if it isn't little..."

"Yep," I cut her off. "It's me! My sister and I loved your caps when we were kids!"

"I know," she laughed, scratching the slightly graying hair on her chin. "You were quite the little scamp! Did you become a hero? How's your mum?"

"Never mind me," I said, looking over her at the glowing coin just a few feet away, in the shallow water. "What did you wish for?"

"You wouldn't believe me if I told you," she said, giggling so giddily that she loosened some phlegm before spitting it out into the fountain. "Lean down, will you?"

I gave a fake grin and knelt. The gnome leaned over to my ear and whispered, "I wished for a tall, handsome, mysterious stranger to come and sweep me off my feet! And you, honey, are the bee's knees!"

Her breath smelled of raw potatoes and some sort of foot cream, so I was already stumbling back. "Whoa there, missy," I said, "I'm already dating the tooth fairy. You'll have to argue with her if you want to stake your claim!"

Nissa gasped. "Oh, no," she said. "I'm not clipping her wings. I just lost a tooth this morning, and I'm hoping for a big payout!"

She laughed again, and I could see the red and swollen gums where the tooth used to be. I was never jealous of Amberfawn's job as the Unremembered Realms tooth fairy. Dealing with people and their rotten teeth would just gross me out.

"You know what would be great?" I asked. "A new dragon cap. Do you still make those?"

Nissa smiled broadly. "You're in luck," she stated happily. "I just opened my shop again a little ways from here. Let me go and grab you one!"

The gnome waddled off, and I quickly turned my attention back to the fountain. "There you are, my little beauty," I said before stepping into the water to retrieve it.

I hadn't heard someone walking up behind me over the shoppers' din and the water's splashing in the fountain. "You're knicked!"

I quickly turned around and saw the worst thing possible. It was Dragondrop Mall Security. I don't know what it's like in your area of the realms, dear reader, but around here, mall security is one of the fiercest and most deadly forces of all. "Were you trying to steal from the fountain?" he asked, tapping his hand with the magical Taze Stick they usually carried. "You trying to pinch other people's wishes?"

"No, officer," I said, holding my hands up. "It wasn't me; I swear!"

He dove at me quickly and hit me with the Taze Stick. Electricity shot through my body, and I started to collapse. The large and powerful security guard caught me and dragged me back out of the fountain. "My coin," I mumbled, still hazy from the effects of his magical weapon.

The security guard threw me to the ground, turned me around, and quickly tied my hands behind my back. "It's okay now, boys," he said to someone. "You can clear the fountain now."

To my dismay, I watched a couple of slimy-looking half-orcs come and start clearing all of the coins out of the pool. "Where you boys headed with all the coins?" asked the guard happily while keeping his foot down on my back.

"Our boss in Neverspring owns the pools in this here mall," one answered. "Elfalfuh is gonna be pleased with this haul!"

I watched them stuff bags full of coins as the security guard hauled me to my feet. "Come with me, hotshot," he said. "Let's get you to the office."

"You got to let me go," I said. "I swear I'll never do it again!"

"That's what they all say," he laughed, shaking his head and pushing me away from the fountain. "For all I know, you might be the infamous Fountain Thief of Farlong."

"I've never robbed a fountain in my life," I lied. "It's bad mojo!"

"Tell it to the mall judge," he stated. "For now, I'm going to stick you in the waiting cell with a creepy little halfling we just picked up.

Under other circumstances, I might have been happy about this. Locked in a cell with Robbie would mean I could finally murder him in peace. But I had a mission to complete, and I didn't want anything else slowing me down. "Do I at least get my one call?" I asked as he led me into the mall's security offices.

"Go ahead," the security guard gruffed.

"YaMacha! Aloonda! Healy, Bok, Choy, Fodderman!" I yelled out into the mall.

A few shoppers turned their heads, but that was about it. There was no way any of my team could have heard me; there were way too many patrons here gabbing and drowning me out. So, the guard pushed me back into the Office of Mall Security and marched me back into a room filled with lockers. He took off most of my items, my rings, cloak, weapons, and poison bandolier and stuffed them into one of the lockers before taking out a key and locking it.

He then led me across the room to a large cage. Inside, was a half-elf, a human, and Robbie the Thief! I grinned as we made eye contact, and so did he, I don't know what he was thinking, but I knew what I was! My dream of finally squeezing the air out of this scoundrel was about to come true! Maybe things weren't going to be so bad after all!

The guard shoved me in the cell and then closed it behind me. With a few words, he cast a magical seal on the lock. "Crud," I thought to myself. "The only type of lock I can't pick."

"A week in here will cool you down," the guard laughed before turning to leave.

"But I've got a job to do!" I yelled to his back as he closed the door to the room. "I'm also in security!"

I turned to Robbie. "If you hadn't stolen my Coin of Cheating, none of this would be happening, you little tick!"

"Finders keepers, you dung wart," Robbie shot back as he leaned calmly against the iron bars. "If you weren't so careless, you wouldn't have lost it in the first place!"

"I was fighting Sand Witches!" I replied angrily.

Robbie looked at me like I was weird. "What? A food fight? What, did a loaf of rye punch you in the breadbasket? If I were there, I would have given it a cold cut combo!"

The halfling laughed at his joke, but I walked up and stuck my finger in his face. "It wasn't a food sandwich. It was some magical desert creatures… never mind, I'm not going to explain myself to someone who is going to be dead in thirty seconds…"

Just then, I felt a tap on my shoulder. "Don't give up hope," a voice said as I quickly spun around.

"Hey," the human said. "We rogues have to stick together."

"Like that's going to help," Robbie said. "Because of this lunatic, my new coin is gone!"

"That's it," I said, "I'm strangling you!"

The human stepped between us. "Listen, you two. Our cellmate, Gacy, has found a way out of here!"

We turned to the pale half-elf, who smiled up at us from his spot. He was on the floor and leaning against a wall. "Tizer is correct," he said in a soft voice. "If you want to get out of here, you'll have to calm down."

There was something I didn't trust about this Gacy character. I couldn't put my finger on it. He looked to be about the creepiest half-elf I'd ever seen. Just the way his beady eyes sparkled made me want to slap him. "You better not be clowning around here, Gacy, I've got a job to do."

"Who cares what you have to do," Robbie butted in. "All I know is I've got a locker out there packed with priceless treasure maps!"

"Really? You have treasure maps?" the human named Tizer asked.

"Yep," Robbie stated as I rolled my eyes. "For the right price, I might sell one to you."

"Don't trust this little runt," I warned him. "He's always pulling scams and getting people killed."

Robbie looked at me angrily, clenching his fist. Then, he calmed down and smiled at Tizer. He raised his small hand and moved it across his chest. "Cross my heart; these are the real thing!"

"Wow!" Tizer said, starry-eyed. "You got yourself a deal!"

"Worry about that later," Gacy cut in. "We've got to get out of this place!"

Reluctantly, I nodded. I had to play along, or I'd never get out of here. Robbie sneered at me and shook Tizer's hand. "Your gonna love all the treasure you find," he began. "Or my name isn't Honest Robbie."

I almost laughed at the little worm, but decided to ignore him. "What's your plan?" I asked Gacy.

"Watch this," he said, moving to one side.

He moved his gloved hand over the wall and pushed on a 3' x 3' brick behind him. It popped open on inset hinges. "A secret door!" Tizer said, smiling. "There is a way out!"

I went over and examined the door. It was top-notch gnoman craftsmanship. "Wow," I said. "This is some quality work! I might not have detected it. How did you find it?"

"I sat here for days," Gacy began. "I kept smelling something rotten and eventually found my way to this brick. It took a bit of fiddling, but I finally figured out how to open it."

"How come you didn't escape earlier?" Robbie asked, peeking into the blackness of a tunnel.

"I was waiting for company," Gacy responded. "There was no way I was crawling in alone. Who knows what's down there!"

"Makes sense," Tizer said. "I think we should give it a shot.

"Who wants to go first?" Gacy asked, looking at the three of us.

We all looked at Robbie, who didn't look happy. "What?!" he said. "Just because I'm small? How heroic of you all!"

"Start crawling, or I'll toss you in!" I said, kneeling and looking him in the eye. "It's your choice..."

He looked at the other two, and they just smiled threateningly in return. "Fine," he said. "But if I get eaten by something, it'll be on your conscience! I hope you can live with yourselves!"

"I'll think about that after I stop laughing," I stated. "Now get in the hole, you rodent!"

Robbie grumbled and crawled in. I was next, then Tizer, and then Gacy, who closed the secret door behind him. It was pitch black, and they probably couldn't see their hand in front of their faces; I could, of course, because my lich eye helped me see things clearly in darkness. I didn't tell any of them that, though. The spacing was tight, but we could easily crawl. The air smelled funny, like something was rotten. The tunnels rocks were damp and cold. "Do you see anything?" I whispered to Robbie.

"Not yet," he replied. "I hope this leads somewhere useful. Backing out would not be fun. I, um, wait a minute, I think I see something!"

We kept crawling, and eventually, we came into a larger room tunneled out of the rock. All four of us stood up and brushed off some dirt. "So far, so good," I stated, looking at the others.

There looked to be two tunnels leading from the room. A small light was coming from both directions, giving the rest of them the ability to see. "I need to get out of here and break back into the security office to get my gear back," I told them. "I hope one of these leads back into the mall."

"I'm sure we'll all be out of here soon," Gacy said, licking his lips. "I can taste freedom..."

He had a bizarre look on his face, and I was beginning to have suspicions about him. "Let's split up," the half-elf said. "Tizer and I will take the left tunnel. You two take the right. We'll meet back here in twenty minutes."

"I'm not going anywhere with this pinhead," Robbie said, pointing to me. "He'll probably wet himself at the first sign of trouble."

"The only thing I'll be wetting is the top of your grave," I shot back. "And maybe adding a little dirt!"

"Shhh," Tizer whispered. "We don't know what's in this place!"

Robbie and I nodded as Tizer waved for us to move along, which we did, reluctantly. Hopefully, there was something down here. I'd give Robbie the coast is clear and send him in first. Maybe whatever monster awaited would be too full to eat me. We walked for a few minutes down the tunnel and then entered a small carved out room like the one we left. Embedded in the room's back wall were small quartz stones with some permanent light spell cast on them. All over the floor of the place was a large variety of skeletons. Humanoids of every race were here, lying in painful, thrashed out positions. "I got a bad feeling about this," Robbie said, kneeling and inspecting a dwarven skull.

"Maybe there's a secret door," I stated, running my hands over a nearby wall. "You check the other side."

We both covered every square inch without finding a thing. "I don't' get it," I stated. "There has got to be a way out."

A loud, piercing scream echoed through the tunnel, and Robbie and I jumped. "That sounded like Tizer," I whispered cautiously. "Let's get over there!"

I grabbed a legbone and broke it in half, giving one part to Robbie, before we dashed back down the tunnel. Soon, we rounded the bend and started down the tunnel where Gacy and Tizer had headed. We arrived in a room just like the one we had left. Piles of bones were all over the floor, but something new was lying with them, Tizer! A mummified husk of his body was on the ground and contorted in what looked to be a painful position. "Where's Gacy?" I said, looking around. "There's no other exit!"

Robbie bent down and poked Tizer on the cheek with his finger. It left a hole. "I've seen this before," Robbie commented.

"So have I," I said, picking up Gacy's gloves off the floor. "The half-elf is a doppelganger."

Doppelgangers are one of the Unremembered Realm's most deadly creatures. They grasp you and suck the life force out of your body, leaving you empty, and then they take on your appearance. The identity thing only lasts a short while, so the creature has to keep feeding every few weeks. I quickly scanned the room again, trying to figure out where the doppelganger was hiding.

Robbie stood up, holding his half of the leg bone in a protective stance. "Do you think he went back up through the tunnel?"

Just as Robbie spoke, a skull came from somewhere off to my right and hit him on the head. The halfling did a few stumbling steps, tripped over some bones, and collapsed on the floor. Sensing the direction of the throw, I scanned with my special vision in that direction. That's when I spotted a small blue light floating in the air. Then, I realized what I was seeing, a magic item! A ring, to be more exact, and it must be a Ring of Invisibility!

I saw the light travel a few more steps, then lower to the ground to pick up another skull. I faked like I couldn't see the creature and dodged when it threw it. After the dodge, I rolled myself in the direction of the blue light, jumped up, and thrust the jagged edge of the broken leg bone into what I hoped was the creature.

A scream erupted from the air in front of me, and the flickering image of Tizer started coming into view. Tizer started changing shapes, once again, and went back to Gacy; then, he finally distorted back into a greenish gaunt creature with blackened eyes and green, foldy, wrinkled skin. The leg bone was embedded in its neck near the collar bone, and blood sprayed from it at least two feet in the air! "Glurgha...mumph...ufghdsc..." was all it managed to mutter before falling flat on its face next to Robbie.

The blood squirted onto the halfling's face, and it woke him up. "Ah!" he screamed, sitting up. "I'm wounded!"

I walked over and knelt beside the doppelganger, pulling the glowing blue ring from its finger. I held it up to Robbie. "It's a Ring of Invisibility," I explained. "He must be in cahoots with security."

Robbie felt around his body, checking for injuries. "Are you telling me he dispensed of the prisoners so the guards can claim all of their gear?" he asked.

"Probably," I stated, slipping the ring on my finger.

"What a scam!" Robbie stated. "I wish I would have thought of that!"

I played with the ring until I figured out how it was activated. I blinked in and out as I rubbed one of the gems on it counterclockwise. "How about we go upstairs, teach the guards a lesson, and grab our stuff?"

We agreed to a plan, crawled back up the tunnel to the holding cell, and peeked out. No one new had been brought in, and the guard was nowhere to be seen. We both pulled ourselves out quietly and got into our planned positions. Robbie was on the floor next to the secret door, which was left open, and I, now invisible, was on the other side of the cell holding Tizer's skull. I banged on the cell bars with the skull until the guard opened the door to the room.

"All right, you mugs, keep it down in here..." he shouted until he saw the bloodied halfling laying on the floor next to the open door. "It can't be!" he said, running over to the cell door.

He mumbled a few words, and the lock clicked. He opened the door and ran over to Robbie. "You should be dead, you little thug," he said, inspecting him.

"Gacy!" he yelled into the tunnel. "Answer me, you freak!"

Robbie immediately bit the guard's ankle as I smashed Tizer's skull on top of his! It was perfect timing. The guard crashed to the floor, completely unconscious. I turned off the ring, knelt over the guard, stuck out my hand, and helped Robbie to his feet. "For once, your good for something!" I laughed.

"I wouldn't say that," Robbie said before biting my hand.

I pulled my hand back and kicked him square in the chest, knocking him backward. I then ran out of the cell and slammed it shut behind me. I heard the click of the normal lock and grinned. He ran to the door and shook the bars. "That was foolish, ghost man," he huffed. "I'm in here with the guard and the keys!"

I just laughed and held them up, giving them a jingle. "Do you think I was just helping you up out of the kindness of my heart?"

"Do you think I just bit your hand for no reason?!" he spat back while holding up the Ring of Invisibility.

The blood coming out of the bite had loosened it so that I couldn't feel it. I watched Robbie blink out, and then I ran over to the locker where I had seen the guard put my belongings. I wish I had time to go through all the lockers, but I knew Robbie would be able to pick the standard lock quickly, so I got my gear on, activated my Cloak of Blending, opened the door, and ran out into the mall into the middle of a crowd of people. Robbie wouldn't be long, so I had to get after those henchmen and quickly!

<hr/>

Chapter 16

"Just where do you think you're going?" YaMacha's voice spoke out as he grabbed my shoulder. "You weren't leaving, were you?"

I sighed and hung my head before turning around. I had barely gotten to the exit doors of the Dragondrop Mall after deactivating my cloak when the big barbarian nabbed me. "I was just going to make a quick run out to get something of mine back," I explained. "It's a slow-moving wagon; I'll be back in a flash!"

"Oh, no, you don't," YaMacha stated.

When I turned around, he was holding a bunch of shopping bags for Aloonda. "I've been following our mage around for the last three hours while you were out here somewhere goofing around! I've even had to hold her handbag!"

Aloonda was smiling and whispered something into Bok's ear, who was standing next to her with his arms crossed. He laughed and repeated whatever it was to Choy, who also started smirking. YaMacha turned around, and all their faces turned serious, again. "But I..." I began to protest.

YaMacha cut me off. "I found out that the interdimensional splinter from the Plane of Death might be in an abandoned mining town called Moonberry. I want to smash it! Understand?!"

I looked at his clenched fist and relented. "Okay, okay. But we have got to hurry!" I complained. "I've got places to go and things to steal!"

YaMacha grinned and patted my head. "Good," he rejoiced. "We're all on board! Do you mind if I put these shopping bags into your magical Sack of Holding?"

"Fine," I groaned, holding out the sack.

When he finished, we all walked out the door and into the bright, hot sun. "My source tells me it's a couple of miles to the Northeast, amongst some mesas and buttes. I guess it's hard to spot, but all we have to do is wait for a zombie to pop out of wherever and follow the footprints."

I could have run off using my Boots of Speeding and Cloak of Blending, but I didn't want to be on YaMacha's bad side, again. That was never worth it. Luckily, he, too, was in a hurry. Something told me he couldn't get away from the mall fast enough. It always amused me that the gigantic man who could practically rip an orc in half-melted like butter whenever Aloonda, the elven beauty, used her feminine enchantments on him. Unlike him, I do what she says because it's in my own interest, not only hers. She sure is pretty, though, and I hate to see her sad. Now, where was I? Oh, yes, the journey to find the interdimensional crack in the butte.

The sun was out high in the sky as we trudged along in the sand. Healy had a handy Divining Wand so that we wouldn't dehydrate, and Aloonda would stand us all back, once in a while, and do a Push Air spell to cool us off. Most of the time, it was just the usual march listening to Bok and Choy discuss trivial nonsense.

"Does a jelly cube monster go to the bathroom?" Bok would start. "And would whatever it leaves be considered jelly drops?"

"I don't think they poo," Choy would reply.

"Everybody does," Bok said back. "If they didn't, that means the jelly cube's brains and their bowel movements are the same."

"They are a magical creature, Bok," Choy mused. "But I must

admit, I've met a few adventurers with droppings for brains."

"Aye," Bok laughed. "I've met a few of those, myself!"

Choy also chuckled, nodding in agreement before Bok asked another question. "Why can't we wear eighteen magic rings at once," Bok inquired. "We could be super powerful!"

"Even magic has its limits," Choy explained. "Who understands the magical magic that makes magic magical!"

"How come scrolls don't' get ruined in water," Bok threw in, ignoring Choy's answer to his first question.

"It's made from magic paper," Choy said, rolling his eyes.

"That's your answer to everything," Bok complained. "Everything is magic. You even said that about my missing sandwich last week!"

"That was magic, too," he replied, before leaning over to me and whispering, "Magically delicious!"

As usual, they began to argue, so I drowned them out of my thoughts by daydreaming of my precious Coin of Cheating—the scene formed in my mind. I'd be in a large gambling hall, with a stack of gold coins piled up on the table, in front of me. Across the table would be Elfalfuh, the elven mob boss, with a matching pile of coins. Surrounding him would be his braindead bodyguards, Apichat and Onquay.

"You got em' this time, boss," Aphicat would say, leaning in close. "There's no way you can lose!"

"That's right," Onquay would echo. "You're much smarter than this foul bit of wind!"

"I'm so confident that I'm going to win," Elfalfuh'd say. "That I'm willing to bet my bodyguards lives on it!"

The two rogue wannabes would, of course, gasp at the statement, but hesitantly and nervously wait for his next order. "Good call, b-b-boss," Apichat would say, trying to slink away, before Elfalfuh'd grab him by the cloak, keeping him at bay.

I'd look around the room at the dozens of spectators, pull out my magic dagger, Magurk, and lay it upon the table. "Here's my wager," I would remark, casually, as the crowd gasped, once again. "So, how do you want to do this? Maybe a coin flip?"

Elfalfuh, of course, would nod in approval as I held out my Coin of Cheating. With a slow-motion flip, it would soon land on the table as he called "Heads." Of course, the coin would land on tails in my favor, because I'd will it. The crowd would cheer, and Elfalfuh would seem unfazed. "Can I call heads now?" I would ask the colossal elf.

The elf would nod, and guards would roll in two guillotines from out of nowhere. The crowd would cheer as the two imbeciles were placed inside of them. "You'll pay for this," Onquay hissed at me as they raised the blade.

"Only if you make a big, bloody mess, and I have to pay for clean up!" I'd laugh as their former boss gave the signal and...

"What are you thinking about," Healy asked, interrupting my daydream. "I've never seen you smile this much."

"Just having pleasant thoughts," I replied. "Sweet, happy thoughts."

"Look!" Bok shouted. "I can see a zombie!"

"This is more like it," YaMacha cheered. "Now we're getting somewhere!"

The zombie had heard us and started coming in our direction. Fodderman, still wearing the horrible dress and with melting eye-liner going into his eye, shuffled off to meet the threat. "I hope there's an army of them!" shouted YaMacha, giddy at the thought of mass destruction.

The zombie was some dead guy in a fancy suit. Most of his hair was gone, and he was missing his lower jaw. When he saw Fodderman in the dress, the zombie raised an eyebrow and straightened out his unkempt bow tie. Before the walking corpse could do anything else, YaMacha ran by him and punched its head clean off. "Yes!" the barbarian laughed as the head rolled off in the sand, eyes still blinking.

The body slumped in the sand and started to twitch. It made me sad that I never got to finish my daydream. I wondered if Api-chat and Onquay would have escaped the guillotine or flopped about the room ruining their boss's furniture. It didn't matter, Ya-Macha was following the trail of footprints, and I had to catch up!

I thought more about my coin as I ran. The thought of one of the half-orc henchmen discovering my treasure disturbed me greatly. While I was on this wild goose chase, they were probably stuffing coins up their noses for a laugh. Half-orcs are like a field of cow droppings; you never know what you're stepping into. One could be smart and cunning, and the other dim and drooling.

How humans and orcs ever end up together never ceased to amaze me. Did they post lonely hearts ads in news scrolls like "Attractive human female, seeks a romantic relationship with smelly, ugly, crud," or were they chance meetups? I couldn't picture a human male raising an eyebrow to an orc female from across the tavern as she cracks a walnut in her hairy armpit! Love finds a way, I suppose. Before I could philosophize any further, YaMacha yelled back to us from a ridge that seemed to have split a mesa in half.

"The footprints lead in here," he yelled happily. "Follow me."

"Go on," Healy said, panting, bent over with his hands on his knees. "I need a breather, and to wait for Fodderman to catch up."

I didn't like the thought of going into a zombie ambush without our cleric, but whatever lied ahead was keeping me from my pursuit of happiness. "I'm going to hit one with my frying pan," Choy laughed as he ran by me.

"You better wash it afterward," Aloonda commented, trotting along after him. "I don't want my eggs to taste like undeath."

She said that while looking at me. I knew my eggs were bad, but that was because I just wasn't a born cook. However, I did wonder if the new secret spice I found would work well on future attempts. I made a mental note, took a deep breath, and entered the crack between the rocks, just behind Bok.

I traveled down the path in the split, surprised at how well-worn it was. I ran my hand along the reddish-brown rock as I hurried. When I walked out of the other side of the crack, I couldn't believe what I was seeing. It was a valley hidden inside a circular ridge of desert stone. The rock walls were at least a couple of hundred feet high, and hot sand covered the ground with no vegetation in sight. As far as I could tell, the crack in the stone was the only way in or out.

"Moonberry," I muttered at the sight of the ghost town.

Dust covered old ramshackle buildings. The doors of every structure had long fallen off, and windows had all been shattered. There was no sign of life there that I could see, and even though we were in a hot desert climate, I got a chill.

Up ahead about fifty yards, I could see Bok, Choy, and Aloonda standing by YaMacha, who was beating a zombie into a pulp. I was just about to run up, but I caught movement in a shadowy doorway of what looked like a dilapidated sheriff's office. I activated my Cloak of Blending and went to my party's right flank. "Howdy strangers," came a voice as a figure stepped out of the shadows.

He appeared to be human, at least six feet tall, and wearing a badge on a worn-out sheriff's tunic. His clothes weren't the only thing worn out, though. His flesh was dried out, and bits of his skeleton showed through. "It's a Shadowhusk," Aloonda said, whispering to YaMacha. "He's a zombie that has retained his mind."

"What brings you folks to Moonberry?" he asked while stepping down the creaky wooden steps of the deck that was falling apart in front of his office.

YaMacha smiled and replied, "We're just here looking to clear out some undead and close a portal to the Plane of Death!"

"Did he just say the Plane of Death, Ange?" another Shadowhusk said, stepping out from behind the Sheriff.

This creature was skinny with two bugged-out eyes and strands of dirty hair hanging over one side of his face. "Don't worry about it, Blarney. We'll work something out."

"Can I use my bolt?" the one called Blarney asked, pulling out a crossbow bolt from a now-empty bolt-sized quiver. "Let me do this; I've been practicing!"

The Sheriff pointed to his partner's foot, to where there was a hole. "C'mon, Ange," he groaned. "That was an accident!"

My party stood in the middle of the sandy street, and I started to have a bad feeling about the situation. "Where is Healy?" I thought to myself, glancing back to the entrance of this remnant of a town.

124

The two Shadowhusks slowly moved ahead a few more feet while my party readied themselves for an attack. Nobody noticed me because of my cloak, so I snuck past my group and made my way toward the two monsters' backs. I didn't know what these undead monsters were up to, but I wanted a good combat advantage.

"Oh, we know where the interdimensional crack from the Plane of Death is," the Sheriff started. "But we don't recommend going through there. Why don't you hang around the town here and have some fun? We're no Hollowood, but we're not totally dead, either!"

"Tell me how many zombies are here, undead lawman…" YaMacha asked while clutching his axe. "Or some heads are going to roll, if you know what I mean."

"We don't' want any trouble," the Shadowhusk sheriff replied. "But I'm afraid we can't let you close that portal. We've got a lot of family and friends wanting back to the plane of the living. We're about to turn Moonberry into an undead hotspot!"

"With picnics, hootenannies, carnivals… you name it!" Blarney cut in, smiling weirdly.

"But the festivities will include eating brains, right?" Choy asked.

"Well, golly," the Sheriff said. "What kind of party would it be without some fresh viddles?"

Blarney took another step forward, wriggled what was left of his nose, and pulled up on his loose-fitting belt. "Now, we do not want any trouble from your group. Let's just get you into a cell while we wait for the others."

YaMacha laughed out loud. "I'd like to see you try! I promise you this- the gang and I will be shooting baskets in the trash can in your office in the next few minutes… with your heads!"

Blarney jumped back behind the Sheriff, peeking out with his buggy eyes and shaking. It was quite comical. Just as YaMacha raised his axe, the Sheriff let out a whistle, and dozens of hands rose from the ground under my party's feet. They pulled them all onto the ground, so that they laid flat and could not move. Dozens of other zombies rose from the sand and started moving toward my group. I slowly began to sneek up behind the Shadowhusk duo when I heard a voice yell out, "Hey! Get away from my group!"

Healy and Fodderman stood by the entry crack, and the cleric's eyes grew big as more than two dozen zombies rose from the ground, moaning and lurching their way toward him. Healy quickly reached into his pack and pulled out his Turning Symbol. "Close your eyes, Fodderman," he said, "this is going to get ugly!"

The zombie did as he was told, and Healy spoke a few magic words while holding up the symbol. Nothing happened. He brought the item down and shook it. "Oh, great," he griped nervously as the zombie horde drew closer. "I left it on again, and it's out of fluid!"

The cleric quickly knelt, reached into his pack, and pulled out a vial filled with some purple liquid swirling inside it. He then unscrewed the top off his Turn Symbol and poured in the fluid. Just as the horde was about to reach him, he held it up and chanted a few words. A purple glow came from the device, turning most of the oncoming zombies into ash. Others ran from it in every direction. During this time, I had gotten close enough to the Shadowhusks and I held Magurk at the ready. I figured a nice blade through the skull might release my captured party members from the horde's clutches. However, just as I raised it, I heard a familiar voice shout out from behind me, in the middle of the road. "I'm back!"

Everyone turned to look and see who had spoken; it was a dark-robed, undead cleric. He had stepped through what looked like a magical, shimmering door that was inset in a rock wall right by us. "Pandermoan," I whispered, finally recognizing him for who he was.

I had killed this evil cleric three times, and I couldn't believe that he had found a way to come back, yet again! I didn't have time to think about anything else, because more figures started coming from the quivering rift that looked like the rock face... it was the portal to the Plane of Death! Dozens of zombies shuffled in behind him, along with some ghouls, and even a few skeletons. I stepped out of the way as Pandermoan approached the Sheriff and Blarney.

"Whoa there, mister," the Sheriff began, "now where do you think you're going?"

Pandermoan laughed and replied. "There's a new sheriff in town," he said, plucking the rusty badge off the real Sheriff's shirt. "Now I'll be giving all the orders around here! Not only that, but…" he trailed off before sniffing the air. "Wait a minute; I smell something familiar here."

My cloak was still on, and I swear he looked right at me, stayed there for a moment, then returned his attention to the Shadowhusks. He spotted my party being held down by all the zombie hands. "It was kind of you to capture lunch for my friends," Pandermoan began. "Let's start crackin' some heads, eh?"

"Hold yer britches," the Sheriff said, placing his hand on Pandermoan's shoulder. "This was our party, and no one invited you!"

With that said, at least fifty or more zombies rose from under the sand, releasing my party and now focusing on the other undead army from the portal as it grew in size. "Now, Blarney," the Sheriff said to his sidekick.

Blarney happily loaded his one crossbow bolt, which he then shakily tried to raise. Before he could move it upward to aim at Pandermoan, it went off, pinning his foot to the ground. He stared at it for a moment, then glanced up to his partner, "Sorry, Ange," was all he could say.

"Rip them to pieces," Pandermoan shouted at his troops as he turned around, walking away from Ange and Blarney. "But save me the female mage. I want to eat her brain all by myself!"

Aloonda, now freed, didn't like the remark and shot a lightning spell in his direction. It fried a few zombies, but Pandermoan had quickly spun about and cast a quick magical shield that deflected the blast. By this time, zombies from both sides were clashing in head-to-head combat, ripping each other's limbs off and biting furiously. I could hear the "bong, bong, bong" of Choy smashing the undead with his frying pan from somewhere in the middle. I could also see writhing corpses being flung into the air as YaMacha dispersed them like weightless dolls!

I knew the barbarian could fight for hours like this, but I also knew he couldn't outlast the endless wave that kept coming out of the Plane of Death. Aloonda was behind Bok, doing her best to attack Pandermoan with her magic. Still, the evil cleric used his magic to stop her efforts, and he'd let a zombie take the brunt of any magical damage she delivered.

By this time, Healy had made it to the rest of us; he still had his Turn Symbol on and was using it to blast away the undead who were trying to kill the Sheriff and his bug-eyed deputy. Fodderman, a much higher quality undead than the rest, tore into other zombies with reckless abandon. The undead fighter knew how to hold his own!

As for me, I only had one target, and that was Pandermoan. Still using my magic cloak to blend, I ducked, dodged, and weaved my way close to the cleric. Unfortunately, I was trampled by a few larger zombies and a half-orc zombie that looked familiar. "Dungbar?" I said, louder than I wanted.

The half-orc zombie turned around and looked in my direction for a moment, as if he remembered something. But he could not see me while I was in blending mode, so he turned around and ran off. I got up and kept moving forward, drawing closer and closer to Pandermoan. By this time, the cleric was getting cocky and doing a shuffle-type dance to taunt Aloonda. "Maybe we'll have a little dance, mage," he laughed. "Before I crack open your pretty noggin' and feast upon your mind! Ha! Who says I don't desire a girl for her brains?!"

Aloonda's anger was kindled, once more, and she tried hitting him with a spell that had a concussive blast. He blocked it, once again. Unfortunately, not only did it hit a few zombies, but me, too! It sent us reeling into the dirt. I felt discombobulated for a moment, but came back to my senses rather quickly. I figured I had gotten close enough to where I could now surprise this fool, so I reached for my Swatfly bow and noticed it was gone! It must have fallen off! I rolled over in the sand to push myself up with my hands and noticed that I was staring at a foot with a crossbow bolt stuck into it.

I grabbed the end and pulled, releasing it from the deputy's foot, as well as the sand. Blarney didn't understand what was going on, because he couldn't see me. Plus, he was trying to fend off an attacking zombie. With the bolt in hand, I jumped up and ran up to Pandermoan, who was blowing a kiss to Aloonda. I dropped my Cloak of Blending and grabbed him by the robe collar. "You!" he croaked. "You're the foulness that I smelled earlier!"

"That's right," I proclaimed happily. "Here's blood in your eye!"

"No, wait!" Pandermoan screamed, but it was too late.

I plunged the bolt through his right eye and deep back into his brain. Goo shot out of his eye socket and splashed over my face before he crumpled to the ground. A magical hiss erupted in the air, and a circular blue burst exploded around me. It didn't affect me at all, but many of Pandermoan's horde screamed out in pain and began running. Some went back into the portal; some ran for the crack, hoping to get as far away as they could. The Sheriff's undead troops, and my party killed the rest.

By the time the excitement had died back down, there were only a couple of dozen Moonberry denizens left milling about with us. "Did you know him?" Ange asked as I poked at Pandermoan's corpse with my boot.

"Sort of," I replied. "The undead cleric is always popping up when I least expect it."

Before I could say anything else, YaMacha marched up and pointed at the portal. "Aloonda, would you have the honor?"

Wiping some blood and blowing some of the hair out her mouth, she smiled and stepped forward. With a few hand gestures and a some garbled words, mud flowed from the rocks above the portal and covered it. Then, with the sweep of her hand, it hardened into rock, once again. "Nice work," Bok said, walking up and tapping on it. "Nothing's coming out of that."

"Let's just hope that the Plane of Death doesn't consume anything else that disagrees with it," Healy said, putting his turn symbol away.

"Wait a minute," I said. "Are you saying this deathly interdimensional rift in space and time has been using Moonberry as some kind of...outhouse?"

"Yup," Healy laughed. "That's what I'm theorizing."

"Poor Dungbar," I said, shaking my head. "He just can't seem to keep out of the sludge."

"Dungbar was here?" Healy asked. "I hadn't seen that traitor since he died back at Stonerow Castle in Moonwink! Was he a zombie?"

"Yeah," I replied. "But I don't see him now; maybe he got turned to ash."

"Or ran off," Bok chimed in. "If I remember right, he's going to be one smelly zombie!"

Sheriff Ange and Deputy Blarney came up to our group with big smiles. "We'd like to thank you for helping preserve Moonberry," the Sheriff began. "Even though we'll miss getting new residents from the Plane of Death, it will be nice having this place get back to normal."

"So you do not want to eat our brains still?" Healy asked.

Ange just shook his head, walked over to Fodderman, and slapped him on the back. "Not when you're partners with a hero like this! We could use him around here; he's so full of life!"

Fodderman let out a groan, and one of his teeth fell out onto the sand. "You know," Blarney stated. "With a little blood, sweat, and fears, we could have Moonberry back to its former glory! What do you say, gang? Can you help us?"

Instead of a group cheer that the dopey deputy expected, we all just stared at him like he was crazy. "No, we won't," YaMacha explained. "But since you did help us fight to stop the portal, I'm willing to let you live, or to not undie, or whatever!"

Sheriff Ange and Blarney whispered into what was left of each other's ears and then turned back to my party. "A truce between the living and the dead," Ange stated, smiling, holding out his hand.

YaMacha shook his hand and said, "Deal."

"Can I go now?" I asked my team. "I did have a previous engagement in Neverspring. Did any of you want to go?"

"We're going to be collecting that reward from the Dragondrop Mall," YaMacha stated. "We'll be sure to set aside your portion."

I was okay with that. The barbarian was brutal and insane sometimes, but he never ripped me off. I hated it when people would try to steal from me. I started to gather my belongings, so I could split, when Aloonda approached me. "You know," she began. "I might be able to teleport you to Neverspring, or at least close to it."

"You have enough magic left in you after that battle?" I asked, worried that she had depleted herself.

"No," she explained, "But I do have a scroll I've been saving for emergencies."

It was settled. My party all decided on the mall, while I would be off in search of my coin. A few minutes later, I was standing in front of a swirling vortex, getting ready to step through. "Are you sure you don't want to come with us?" Choy asked.

"I've got a promise to keep," I stated, trying to be noble. "Besides that, I don't want to be inside the Dragondrop Mall when Aloonda gets her share of the reward; you guys will be shopping for days!"

With that said, I could see their faces drop; Aloonda gave me a wink. Then, I quickly jumped through the portal and into blackness. As the doorway of the portal faded out, I could see YaMacha frantically trying to run over to the doorway. "Wait for me!" he cried out, but it was too late; I was gone.

Chapter 17

Teleporting is such a bizarre experience. I know traveling in-between time and space only lasts for a second or two, but it always gives me the feeling that I'm falling in pure blackness for much longer. It also seems to drain me of energy for some reason and makes me hungry. Before I could think about it any further, a portal opened ahead and pushed me through. It took my eyes a second to adjust, so I rubbed them, hoping to clear them of any blurriness. The smell of death and fire instantly hit me, and I coughed at the acrid fumes. "What in the realms?" I asked out loud to no one in particular as I surveyed the landscape.

The dozens of bodies that laid scattered around me came into focus. Then, my gaze shifted to a burning wagon with a few dead half-orcs laying around it. It was Elfalfuh's men! Aloonda had sent me to the exact location I needed to be! I walked over and observed bite marks all over them. The many bodies of the fallen undead surrounding them pretty much gave away who the culprits were. By the way, if you kill an undead, is it now dead dead, or redead, or unredead? That's something that's always boggled me. I made a mental note to ask Choy about this, but I already knew what his answer would be.

As I looked over the carnage, I noticed that the bodies weren't just of half-orcs and zombies; there were lizardmen and clerics of every race, too! "Wait a minute," I thought to myself.

I knelt at a zombie and took a sniff. My guess was correct; it reeked of sewage and coffee! This poor sap was one of Undead Society's poets! He even had a moldy beret! I ran over to a dead cleric and saw that he wore the sigil of the Temple of Gallowman. Lying next to him was a lizardman with a crushed skull. It looked as if it had been clobbered with a mace. I couldn't believe it; it was one of the same lizardmen that Froghat had said he would chase down with the other flea brains of our party!

It slowly dawned on me that the wagon, carrying all the gold and my coin, must have converged with the still-fighting clerics and undead poets. Not only that, but they must have bumped into all those lizardmen and their Chamelion.

I quickly did a scan with my lich eye to see if the horrible beast was still around, but I didn't see it. I jogged over to the over-turned wagon and searched whatever was not on fire, but I had no luck; my Coin of Cheating, along with the other gold, was missing! I kicked the side of the wagon in frustration and started pacing amongst the corpses. What had happened here? Who took off with the treasure? How do I find them? I took some deep breaths and tried to calm myself down. "Somebody had to live," I said out loud to myself. "And that means someone left, and if they left, then there are footprints!"

As I started inspecting for tracks in the terrain, I realized that Froghat and the gang were not among the bodies. I confirmed my suspicions when I spotted a dead lizardman with a thick green bogey wiped on its forehead. "Pickenfling," I said, frowning. "How could they have survived?"

But then, I spotted a more significant clue. There was a gray hairball not far from the same body. After a closer inspection, I knew it was a goopy mix of Froghat's hair and Ozone the Frog's stomach acid. I looked around the ground and saw footsteps in the dirt that seemed to lead south. That's when I realized that they had, not only survived, but also went to Froghat's private cabin not-too-far from here. I knew where that was, so I did not hesitate and ran as fast as possible to reach the kooky wizard and the others.

When I got within one hundred yards of the cabin, I could hear the barking laugh of DogChauw. As I moved forward, I could see him, Stretch Markus, Pickenfling, and Froghat, all sitting around a campfire, eating. On the spit, roasting above the fire, was a big chunk of meat. When I got closer, I could smell it, and it was wonderful!

"Gwai Lo!" they all cheerfully shouted as I walked up.

"We're glad you came back," Stretch Markus said, with food stains surrounding his mouth. "We thought you went to Miftenmad."

"Yeah," Pickenfling added, after a long belch. "Did you ever find Skole?"

"Yes, I did," I explained. "But things didn't work out as I had hoped."

They offered me a big chunk of the meat they were all eating, so I accepted and ate ravenously. "What happened with you guys?"

"Well," Froghat explained. "We decided to follow the lizard-men around, hoping to catch them at a weak moment. Then, whammo! We struck!"

"It took a couple of days," Dogchauw continued. "But then, we saw our chance."

"So you struck them at night, stabbing backs and killing with no second thoughts?" I asked before taking another bite.

"No," Froghat laughed. "We found the remnants of a battle

and then looted the bodies for treasure. Just like you taught us!"

I finished chewing, swallowed, and asked. "Wow. You actually listened to me, for once. So, was there much treasure?"

They all laughed, then held up some coin sacks, which looked wonderfully full. "Come inside the cabin, Gwai Lo," Froghat said. "I'll show you a real special treasure!"

I was hoping it would be my coin, so I got up and followed him through the doorway. His cabin looked like it did the last time I had seen it; a mess. It was a run-down bachelor pad with magic components strewn about the place. It smelled like off cheese, and there were a variety of frog tanks sitting on counters throughout the house. Froghat shouted, "Surprise!" and pointed with both hands to a mounted animal head on the wall. I couldn't believe it; it was the head of the Chamelion!

"How did you kill that?!" I replied, totally shocked.

The wizard let out a chuckle and struck a spellcasting pose. "Let's just say that no creature is ferocious enough to withstand the powerful magic of Froghat!"

"It was dead when you got to battle, wasn't it?" I said, not believing a word of what I just heard.

"Well," he responded in a calm tone. "There might have been a little twitching going on. So, I made sure to blast him good with one of my specials."

He held his fingers out like they were zapping something, but I just rolled my eyes and decided to get down to business. "Listen," I explained. "I have lost a special coin, and I'm trying to retrieve it. I believe it's in one of those sacks of gold out there. I need it back."

"How did you lose it?" Froghat asked. "Tell me the whole story, right from the beginning."

"I haven't got time," I said.

"Did you bring my secret Thieves Guild pin?" he asked before whispering, "I never gave our secret away."

"Not yet," I replied, looking at his now disappointed face. "But I did bring a gift!"

I reached into my pocket and pulled out a sheet of paper. "It's an autograph from Snails & the Marshtunes!" I exclaimed, trying to remember their name from one of their tour flyers.

"Marshtones," Froghat corrected me, a huge smile crossing his face. "This is fantastic! Thank you!"

The wizard took the paper, embraced it, looked again, and then embraced it, once more. I never understood what the big deal was. After all, it was just another band of bards that played in cheap dives. After calming down, Froghat started humming a Scales song and making some tea, as if this would be an extended visit. "Listen," I told him, fighting back my frustration. "Let's just go through the coins, okay?"

Froghat shrugged and smiled, "Okay. Let's go through the gold!"

After explaining the situation to the others, they all poured out their treasure sacks and started sifting through them. After twenty minutes or so, I realized that the coin was not there. "I don't get," I said, exasperated. "If this were all the treasure, it would have to be in here!"

"What about the Gallowman Clerics," Pickenfling stated. "Maybe they have it."

"What is he talking about?" I asked, turning to Froghat. "What clerics?"

Froghat looked as if he just realized something and stuck his finger in the air. "That's right!" he proclaimed. "We donated some of our gold to their temple. It was the least we could do after hearing about the tragedy at their place."

"What did they look like?" I asked, getting hopeful, again.

Stretch chuckled. "They were the chubbiest dwarves I've ever seen. They had so many crumbs in their beards that I could have guessed their last five meals."

"I know those two!" I said, excited. "Knowing their state of health, I may just be able to catch up to them before they get back to their temple!"

I was just about to take off running, but Pickenfling held up his hands, "Whoa there," he started. "They didn't go back to their temple."

"What?" I asked. "Where would they go?"

"After receiving the bag of gold, they wouldn't stop talking about making a quick visit to the new Doubledeal Casino located outside of Mound Doom," Froghat explained. "I guess they needed to bless it or something."

"They sure looked happy," Stretch said. "It gives you a warm feeling, helping out clerics in need. Can I get an amen?"

I took off so fast the nitwits probably fell over from the breeze I left. I had a couple of clerics to catch, and I had to hurry before they gambled my coin away! It could be even worse, though, I thought; what if they discovered how useful my coin could be at a casino! The sun was starting to set in the sky, so I activated my Cloak of Blending. I didn't want any wandering monster slowing me down or eating me before I got my coin back!

As I moved through the forest on my way to Mound Doom, I spotted a blue dragon at the mouth of its cave, feasting on a group of dead adventurers. I hated seeing this, but it was a reminder that I had to be careful as I traveled. Death is common in the Unremembered Realms, because of all the dangers, but if you play your cards right, you can live to a ripe old age. I never wanted to be a snack for something or to be snuffed out by an executioner. I hoped to die in bed with my boots on, clutching a bag of gold, and throwing my dagger one last time at some dumb druid passing by.

After running for a bit, I decided to verify my position by climbing a tree. I was able to get high enough to peer over the treetops. It was now dark, so I could see the Doubledeal Casino's lights off in the distance. If I ran as fast as I could, I would probably make it there in about twenty minutes or so. I was just about to climb down when I heard two voices just below me.

"How much you think we're going to make, Grifft?" one said.

"I don't know, Baroosh," the other replied. "We'll find out when the dragon is done eating."

They both started giggling. "Could you imagine the look on the fool's faces when they stepped into the cave looking for safety, and they ended up staring a blue dragon in the face?" the one called Grifft guffawed.

"I hope them filling their trousers didn't ruin the taste for old

136

bluey!" Baroosh laughed. "Those brainless clods!"

From the awful way they were dressed, it looked like these two were a couple of druids. "It'll probably nap after it eats, then we can go search the remains for anything good," the skinny, balding one named Grifft remarked.

Great, I thought. I can't be stuck up here waiting for these two knuckleheads. I dreaded the thought of having to listen to boring conversations about druidy stuff, like the amazing color of dirt, or what to name your head lice. I pondered my situation for a minute and came up with a plan. I donned my hat of disguising and made myself appear as a scarred up half-orc. Then, I called down below. "Would you two keep it down? I'm trying to rest!"

Shocked, the two druids jumped back and pulled out a couple of daggers. "Whoa, there, buddy boys," I said, hopping down from the tree onto the ground. "I'm just a rogue, like you two."

"How did you see through our disguises?" the one called Baroosh asked.

"Just now," I replied. "One, your daggers, and two, you don't smell."

"What did you hear, half-orc?" Grifft asked as he backed up a step.

"Enough to know I wouldn't want to tangle with such powerful minds as yours," I said, holding back laughter. "What a genius plan!"

"Who are you?" Baroosh asked. "And why shouldn't we just kill you where you stand?"

I made up a name on the spot. "My name is Burgle," I lied. "I was on my way to the Doubledeal Casino to rob it. I wasn't looking for trouble."

"Good luck with that," Grifft grunted. "We tried robbing it twice and failed. The security is way too tight."

Baroosh shook his head. "They chased us out," he further explained. "It's a shame, too. A couple of overweight dwarves were having a lucky night, and we were going to rob them! Then, these two beautiful female bounty hunters ruined our plans, but lucky for us, we found a party of rubes on our way north. They had some nice armor. Hopefully, the dragon didn't damage it, too much."

Suddenly, we heard some voices coming from the south. "Oh, no," Grifft whispered loudly. "That sounds like the ones who chased us out of the Doubledeal! What do we do?"

"Quick," I said to the duo. "Climb up my tree, and I'll see who it is. Don't worry; you can trust me, or my name isn't Burgle!"

"You are a good one, Mr. Burgle," Baroosh stated while shaking my hand. "I promise you a bit of our treasure."

I watched the two scramble up the tree. I would have helped, but I didn't feel like it. As soon as the two were up and quiet, two female fighters came into view on the trail. The hair on my neck stood up when I realized that it wasn't just two ordinary fighters; it was Sunshine and Moonbeam, the most gorgeous and deadly bounty hunters in all the Unremembered Realms! I almost broke off into a run, but I remembered that I was wearing my Hat of Disguising, and they probably wouldn't recognize me. "Evening, ladies," I casually said as they approached. "Lovely night, eh?"

Sunshine looked me over for a moment. "Have you seen a couple of ugly druids around here?" she asked.

"Yep," I replied. "They are hiding up in that tree!"

"What!" one of the rogues yelled before slipping out of his place.

We heard a crack, and a couple of hollers, as Baroosh and Grifft fell onto the ground with a few broken branches. Sunshine and Moonbeam immediately went over and twisted their arms behind their backs before binding them. "You, you, traitor!" Baroosh yelled, looking up at me. "How could you do this!"

"Yeah," Grifft added. "Why would you turn us in?!"

"For the reward," I happily stated. "I'm sure these lovely ladies have some coins they are offering for information on your capture. Am I right?"

Sunshine picked Grifft up and shoved him back toward the trail before walking up to me. She handed me a small stack of coins and smiled. "Thank you, mister...um.."

"Burgle," I replied. "Burgle is my name."

"No, it isn't!" Baroosh shouted as Moonbeam got him to his feet. "He's lying!"

Moonbeam stomped on his foot with her silvery metal boot and he cried out in pain. "Nice work, Burgle," she said, flashing me a perfect smile. "Are you a bounty hunter, too?"

"No, no," I laughed. "Just a simple half-orc, trying to bring some justice into the realms."

"He's a rogue," Grifft cut in. "An untrustworthy one at that!"

"An untrustworthy rogue?" Sunshine laughed. "There's a shocker!"

Moonbeam laughed, too, then approached me, as well. "Rogue or not," she said. "You did well. I've got a good feeling about this one."

Then, she pulled out a scroll and opened it, showing me a wanted poster with a sketch of my undisguised face on it. "If you ever run into a fellow rogue who looks like this," she explained. "Detain him, and you'll get a reward you wouldn't believe!"

I pretended to study the face. "Not a problem," I stated. "I don't know what a handsome fellow like that could have done to have such a high bounty, though."

"Don't get us started," Sunshine said, shoving Grifft back down the trail toward the casino. "We'd be here all night!"

Moonbeam gave me a wink, and I swear I got light-headed. Their beauty was truly intoxicating and it was not easy to resist the urge to confess, so that they could arrest me, as well! They did have this effect on many of the male creatures in the realms, and I had to snap myself out of the daze their charms put me in. Perhaps it was the sack of gold coins in my hand that helped. I always enjoyed that more than anything! "Now, for their treasure," I whispered to myself.

After they left, I quickly jogged back to where the dragon cave was and looked over the remains of the gullible party that the rogues had duped. This party may not have been much in the brains department, but they were top-notch cuisine for the now, full, and sleeping blue dragon that I could hear snoring.

I gingerly picked over the party's pieces and took over two hundred gold coins, a nice set of magic scale mail armor, a glowing sword, and a unique looking set of bracers. As usual, I didn't want to carry all this stuff, so I hauled it off deeper into the woods and dug a hole. If Aloonda hadn't stuffed my magical Sack of Holding with all her shopping, I could have easily just brought this all with me! But there was no way I was going to ditch all her new clothes!

It took over an hour, but I didn't want anyone to find this bit of loot that I just claimed. I marked its location on my special journal map and got back on the trail after a swig of water and a few crumbles of bread. I kept in disguise and started running, again. I hoped the dwarves were still there, gambling, which I believed they would be. After all, they had my Coin of Cheating!

<hr />

Chapter 18

It didn't take long to reach the Doubledeal Casino. The lights coming from the large, magically illuminated marquee made it appear like a lighthouse amongst a sea of trees. Flashing gold, green, blues, and purples lit up the night sky, beckoning one and all to come gamble away all their hard earned wages. There were smiling couples walking in with high hopes and others walking out with despair in their eyes.

I wondered how many of these poor sots even saved enough coin for a one-way ride to Desperation Point, where they'd finish their swan song of life with a swan dive! Once in a while, though, a lucky patron would come out hollering with delight, letting half the realms know about their lucky streak and big winnings. I felt bad for them, too. I figured every rogue or ne'er-do-well within a half-block would be following them home, more than willing to help relieve them of all that heavy gold. I took note of this, realizing that the real jackpot was waiting for chumps to come outside.

LaFarina, the mob-connected owner of the Doubledeal, was known for not caring whether her customers were robbed of all their riches later. Rumor had it that she was usually the one hiring the thugs who robbed the soft-headed fools who thought they could walk out with a big chunk of her money. LaFarina was small, even for a halfling, but feared nothing and tended not to let anyone get in her way. If I was going to get my coin back, I had to keep my head low.

"Traitorous swine!" I heard a voice yell out the moment I walked through the door. The entire place fell silent as they looked at me.

Across the room were Grifft and Baroosh, being handed over to LaFarina, herself. The halfling snapped her fingers and guards brought out sacks of gold for Moonbeam and Sunshine, who both gave me a small wave before turning around and accepting their reward from LaFarina's men. I smiled and waved back as they left the casino, obviously on to their next job. I didn't know what would happen to the two rogues, but I didn't care. I started to search the other areas of the casino.

Hundreds of humanoids of all races filled the place. One of the things that always amazed me about the Unremembered Realms' beings is that for all the divisiveness, killing, and class warfare, there was still something that brought everyone together-greed. From the slimy-looking kobolds playing cards and spitting on each other to the group of human nobles tossing some dice just a few tables away. Places like this brought everyone together. "Watch where you're going!" hissed an old lady with blue hair after walking straight into me, "Are you blind?!"

She adjusted her thick glasses before hobbling off, again. I checked my pockets to make sure she wasn't a top-level thief using a disguise. After all, sometimes things are not as they appear, here in the realms. Nothing was missing, so I placed the diamond brooch that I had nicked into a side pouch and kept moving. As I made my way into another section, I looked around for the two dwarves.

The place was packed, making them hard to spot. Especially, since there were so many other dwarves. I thought I would check out the Complaint Department, because that's where most of the short, gruff humanoids liked to hang out. "I want my money back or another dice throw at the table," a black-bearded dwarf demanded while pounding his fist on the counter in front of the window. "It's too hot in here, and that caused my arthritis to flare up.

It goofed up my roll!"

"Next," was all that the large, bored-looking woman said from behind the counter. "Next, please."

Normally, I could watch this for hours. I loved it when grumpy dwarves were dealt with like this. Mind you, I do like dwarves. I get a lot of amusement from watching their misery! "I lost at the card table ten times in a row," the next one griped. "That's too many. Your casino is rigged. Furthermore..."

"Next," the lady stated again, without a single bit of emotion.

The dwarf stormed off in a huff, with his face beet red. I chuckled and shook my head. The line was clear now, so I decided to talk to the lady to determine if the two dwarves had been there recently. "Have you seen two dwarves?"

She stopped filing her nails for a minute, looked me up and down, then said, "You're kidding me, right?"

"No," I said. "The duo are clerics, kind of on the heavy side, with food stuck in their beard."

"That's every dwarf in this place," she said, not looking up. "Next."

"If you would just listen," I started to say.

"Scram, you half-orc dimwit," a dwarf behind me stated. "I lost a lot of coin here tonight, and I've got a lot of complaining to do!"

The voice sounded familiar. As I stepped out of the way, I turned around and spotted my on-again-off-again travel companion, Badwigg. "Hey Badwigg," I blurted, out of habit. "Nice haircut."

He wasn't in his usual scale armor, but a cheaply made tux that a funeral parlor probably sold off after all the loved ones left. The dwarf's hairpiece was new, though he had forgotten to remove the price tag, again. The wavy brown toupee sat twisted on his head, probably due to him pulling on it in frustration. "How do you know my name, half-orc?"

"That's your name?" I said, trying to cover my tripping of the tongue. "How appropriate!"

"What is that supposed to mean!" Badwigg shouted, angrily.

142

The dwarf started hurling insults at me as he tried to straighten out his toupee, but I left quickly, chuckling at how easy it was to press his buttons. It didn't matter. I didn't have time to chitchat; I had to find out if anyone had seen the dwarven clerics. I heard the clickety-clack scramble of the marble on a roulette wheel, so I made my way to where the sound came from and watched it land on a number. Multiple groans arose as the croupier, or tablejockey, as I called them, used a hooked stick to clear all the losing bet coins into a hole in the table. "I bet that's full," I thought to myself, a grin growing on my face.

"Place your bets, place your bets," the tablejockey yelled as he picked the marble up from the wheel. "Pick your numbers, pick your numbers!"

I pulled a handful of gold coins from my pocket and placed it all on 11, which happened to be my lucky number. Then, I moved as close to the wheel as I could to get the best view of the spin. A small crowd gathered and watched as the white marble bounced around the wheel until it eventually settled on 18, for a moment. Then, with the flick of my minor telekinesis power, the marble jumped onto 11. The crowd let out a cheer as the frowning table-jockey pushed a stack of gold my way. Which, I immediately moved back over onto 11.

"That's a bold move, handsome," the sultry voice of a female said from behind me.

"I'm a bold guy," I replied, turning around to see the female half-orc standing behind me.

She wore a shiny dress, had matted long black hair, and her chin was red and blotchy from where she must have freshly plucked out some hair. I could have kicked myself for picking this disguise. "Do you mind if I watch next to you?" she said, strolling up.

I don't know what kind of animal died making her perfume, but it reeked of sour cabbage and dog food. "I'm Ugmug," she said, giving me a wink. "What's your name?'

"Burgle," I stated. "Justice Burgle. Nice to meet you."

The marble dropped again and eventually landed on a 3, but

before the crowd could groan, I made sure it popped up and landed on 11, once more. The crowd held up their arms and cheered even louder this time, drawing everyone else's attention in the room. When the perturbed croupier shoved even more gold my way, I boldly pushed it onto 11, yet again. "I must be your lucky charm," Ugmug said, staring at my gold. "I sense something different about you. You're more than what you seem!"

People swarmed around my table to see if my number would go again. If I got out of here alive, I'd have to get Badwigg the Cleric to heal me of my back issues from hauling all this gold! Still, I was getting a bit nervous from all the attention. The tablejockey dropped the marble, once again, and everyone watched it spin. "I just know you're going to win," Ugmug exclaimed. "You're going to be even luckier than the two dwarven clerics in the next room!"

"What?!" I asked, turning to her. "What did you say?!"

"23!" shouted the tablejockey.

A collective groan came from the crowd and a big frown formed on the poorly lipsticked lips of Ugmug. "I'm going back to the dwarves!" she said. "You, sir, are not all that!"

I was certainly relieved at those words. If there was ever a time in my life that I didn't want to be all that, this was it! The less-than-attractive half-orc made her way through the crowd with me not far behind. We made it through a couple of busy rooms filled with hundreds of other gamblers. There was a lot to see, but the one thing consistent in each room was the wanted posters of yours truly hanging about every six feet on every wall. I was sure most of the gamblers here would love to get their greedy mitts on me to turn over to Sunshine and Moonbeam. The reward was certainly large enough to keep them losing at the Doubledeal for many a moon. I figured I had better keep my disguise on for a bit longer.

Suddenly, there came a loud, angry roar of people as I entered the final room of the south end of the casino. Standing on a gambling table, was a large guard and the two dwarven clerics. The guard was holding my Coin of Cheating up in the air. "These two have been using some kind of magical coin to cheat," he yelled. "The Doubledeal Casino will not tolerate dishonesty!"

The crowd let out a cheer and started booing and hissing at the dwarves. "We didn't know it was magic!" cried out one of the dwarves. "We were trying to make some gold for our temple. It was attacked by evil poets!"

The crowd booed even louder after hearing that, but it was all hushed by a loud whistle. Everyone turned to look as LaFarina, herself, was carried on the shoulders of a large human barbarian to the table where the dwarves stood. When she climbed down off his shoulders, she addressed the crowd. "Does everyone here know the punishment for deception?"

The crowd cheered. Then, LaFarina pointed to the northeast and shouted, "Throw them both into Mound Doom, along with their cheating coin!"

"Mound Doom! Mound Doom! Mound Doom!" the crowd bellowed over and over, again. Then, they hauled the dwarves down from the table and guided them through the crowd. I did not know what was going to occur or how. But, I did know that I had to stop them before they threw my precious coin into boiling lava. Oh, yeah, and the dwarves, too.

Chapter 19

I tagged along with the crowd on the way to Mound Doom. It was easy to blend in with so many people going to watch the two dwarves meet their fate. I thought most of these die-hard gamblers wouldn't leave the casino, but that was a wrong assumption, because they were taking bets and guessing odds along the way. "I say the lava will consume them in five seconds or less," a large-nosed gnome shouted.

"I bet they'll both evacuate their bowels at the same time," cackled an elderly woman with an eye patch. "Right before they are shoved off!"

"Give me 3-to-1 on the lava and 6-to-1 on the bowels," a greasy-haired bandit said. "Tonight's my lucky night!"

The old woman turned to me and asked, "What about you,

stranger, you willing to bet?"

I pondered the situation for a moment, and then asked, "What are the odds on the dwarves escaping?"

The group snickered and the woman replied, "100-to-1," before spitting on the ground. "Are you in?"

I reached into my magical Sack of Holding, pulled out 25 gold coins, and handed them to the old bird. "Let's hope for a glorious escape, eh?" I said. "I think those two slobs could surprise us all!"

The others just laughed, but I didn't mind. They had no idea what I'd do to save my coin, I mean, the dwarves from their predicament. It wasn't long before the crowd stopped walking up the mound's slow incline and gathered in a half-circle around the top of Mound Doom. The heat rising from the center of it was intense. Beads of sweat began to form on my brow, and I wasn't even close to the edge! I could hear the lava as it percolated. Each fiery bubble that slowly burst let out a slurping sound and then a hiss. It reminded me of my stomach after eating the mystery meals at Ol' Shrively's Tavern.

"Welcome, one and all," LaFarina shouted from the shoulders of the barbarian. "I hope everyone has made their bets by now."

The crowd cheered in approval while the two clerics were prodded up to the edge of Mound Doom. Sweat poured off of them as they nervously looked around. "No last meal?" one of them asked.

"Yeah," the other one agreed. "How can you be so cruel to send us off on an empty stomach?"

"Well, give us a minute," LaFarina replied. "We're about to have a fry up!"

The gamblers all roared out in laughter as the halfling crime boss climbed off the barbarian. She began pacing in front of the crowd and started ranting and raving about some nonsense. I wasn't listening; I was trying to come up with some kind of plan. That's when she pulled my Coin of Cheating from her cloak and held it up in the air. It glimmered in the lava light, making it that much more beautiful! The crowd let out ooh's and aah's and seemed to be transfixed by it. That's when it hit me, a cunning plan!

146

With the crowd distracted, I took off from the central cluster and activated my Cloak of Blending. I also removed my Hat of Disguising; that way, the dwarves would recognize me and know I was there to help. I was glad it was so dark and shadowy in the crowd; it would have been a lot harder to pull this off in broad daylight. "Spudgum and Tate are going to meet their fate tonight, all because of their greed and this coin!" LaFarina shouted.

The crowd seemed to hang on to her every word. "I hope they learn their lesson," she continued, "as the fat melts off their rumps!"

"I'm still hungry," Spudgum mumbled.

I had snuck in close enough now that I could hear him. I padded just behind LaFarina as she continued to address her audience. "Let this be a lesson to all of you out there," the halfling lectured, holding the coin above her head, "That nobody double deals the Doubledeal!"

With that said, I deactivated my Cloak of Blending and plucked the coin from her hand. "I'll take that, if you don't mind," I said before turning to the two dwarves. "Run!"

Spudgum and Tate looked at me in surprise; so did everyone else there. "Hey," someone shouted from the crowd. "It's the thief from the poster! He's worth a fortune!"

I kicked LaFarina in the backside and turned to run as she flew forward onto the grass. Then, I felt two large arms circle around me that started to squeeze! I had already anticipated this and flung my dagger into his left foot! The barbarian screamed out in pain and let me go. I immediately grabbed my weapon and pulled it back out before turning to run. That's the exact moment that I was tackled and flew backward toward the edge of the mouth of Mound Doom! The person who had attacked me wrestled with me trying to get the coin from my hand. It was the greasy-haired bandit who I had been walking with earlier!

"Give me the coin," he spat, "it's mine!"

I slugged him hard in the stomach before giving him an uppercut with my lizardman hand. This blow toppled him over the edge, but luckily for him, he grabbed my tunic's sleeve, pulling me down, as well. Things went so fast that I hadn't noticed that he had gotten ahold of the Coin of Cheating and held it in his right hand, while he used his left one to hold onto my clothing. The bandit's eyes grew wide as he slipped a little, letting his legs hang dangerously close to the lava. "Drop me," he shouted, "and you'll lose the coin, too!"

From behind me, I could hear LaFarina shouting at her barbarian guard, "Kill them! Kill them!"

Thankfully, none of the gamblers were willing to jump in on this skirmish. They seemed to be more interested in placing bets on everything happening. "My foot hurts, woman!" he sobbed. "I've got an owwie!"

"Fine!" she screamed, "I'll do it, myself!"

I glanced over just in time to see her get tackled by Spudgum and Tate! "Hurry, rogue," Tate yelled. "We've got to get out of here!"

The crowd of onlookers still did not move a muscle. That's when I heard the old lady I met earlier shouting out new odds. "They're taking bets on you dying!" I said to the bandit, still dangling. "They are not in your favor!"

"My gang are out there," he hissed back. "They won't let me die just to make a few coins!"

Then, a look of realization crossed his face, "I'll kill those slimebags!"

"Just give me my coin, and I'll pull you up," I said, struggling not to be pulled over the edge. "It's very precious to me!"

"No," he screamed. "It's mine! My men will be here in a minute to rescue me; then you'll be sorry!"

That's when a voice rang out from the crowd, "Hurry up and die, DaFizzle! I've got a fiver with 10-to-1 odds you become a wad of charcoal!"

My tunic sleeve ripped, and the bandit fell a few inches. The sleeve was only holding him up by a few threads. DaFizzle shot me a look of disdain and then grinned at me. "If I can't have it," he stated. "Then, nobody will!"

With that said, he let go and held up the coin, just out of my reach. An insane smile crossed his face, but it didn't last, because I used my telekinesis to pull the coin from his hand. The last thing DaFizzle saw before hitting the lava was the Coin of Cheating floating up to my awaiting palm and the big smile on my face.

I stood up quickly and turned to face the crowd. Half of them cheered, and the other half groaned, as I held up the coin victoriously. Immediately money changed hands. "Get your hands off me, you filthy dwarves!" LaFarina yelled as Spudgum and Tate got her to her feet.

"You going to toss her over?" I asked the duo.

"No," Spudgum stated. "We're clerics, not barbarians."

With that, Tate punched her in the face, knocking her out. "But that doesn't mean we're not gonna flatten this wretch!"

The large barbarian was still groaning. "My foot hurts, cleric. Can you heal me?"

I would have laughed in his face, but Tate replied. "Sure, but you have to let us go and take your boss back to where she belongs!"

"I can only promise severe torture," he spat. "But I'll make sure LaFarina doesn't kill you."

"What about the rogue and his coin?" Spudgum asked.

"He'll get what he deserves," the barbarian growled. "Now heal me!"

The onlooking crowd immediately began shouting out numbers and exchanging money. Would the dwarves heal the barbarian to save their necks? Or would they run and hope he doesn't hunt them down and slaughter them like most other barbarians are known for doing. The two dwarves appeared nervous and looked at me with large eyes, hoping I could help.

Then, an idea hit me. "Listen," I said, stepping up to the barbarian. "I'm a master of escape. There's no way you could catch me, even if you wanted. I'm even willing to bet on it!"

The crowd started shouting out numbers, once again. "I'm so confident that I'm willing to give you my last potion of healing," I said to the musclebound goon. "As long as you let these two go."

The barbarian thought for a moment, sizing me up. "It's a

deal," he sneered. "You have my word."

I've been adventuring a long time, and I knew for certain this was a lie. I would not be here today if I hadn't mastered the technique, myself. As some say, "It takes one to know one."

I nodded in agreement, took a vial from my bandolier, and tossed it to him. He looked at the label and smiled. "Healing," he read.

He flipped out the cork and guzzled it down before saying, "That was a huge mistake on your part, rogue."

Spudgum and Tate both looked at me, "You should run," Tate said nervously.

"What," I replied, "and miss the show? That was a vial of brain-melting poison."

"Poison?!" the barbarian shouted. "But, you, the label said..."

"I always switch the labels," I laughed. "They teach that in Rogue 101."

"This is terrible!" someone shouted from the crowd. "I had 100 gold on the barbarian!"

"You think?!" the barbarian yelled before grabbing his throat as his eyes started bugging out.

I don't think I'm going to describe what happened next, but I am happy to inform you that the brain-melting poison wasn't an exaggeration! "I've got to get more of that!" I said to the dwarves as the barbarian hit the ground, face first.

"Thanks for the rescue," Tate said, shaking my human hand. "Oh, and go ahead and keep that coin. It seems to be a lot of hassle."

"You two rescued me back outside the temple," I said. "Let's just call it even, shall we?"

"We're not out of the woods, yet," Spudgum stated while a handful of the gambling people approached. "Grab your dagger."

We all stood at the ready as a group of bandits drew near. One held up his hand. "No need to be worried," he explained. "We'd like to ask if you'll join our gang."

"You don't want to turn me in for the reward?" I asked. "Plus, I'm kind of thinking you want revenge for the death of your friend."

"Are you kidding?" another one chimed in. "You wouldn't have such a high price tag if you weren't super skilled. You know, we could use someone like you in the House of MaHizzle."

"DaFizzle was our captain, but it seems like you have a lot more to offer," another one commented. "What do you say?"

They were not very friendly-looking, and I wanted to get the dwarves away and retain my coin at the same time. "Sure," I agreed. "But on one condition."

"What's that," one said.

"See that old lady?" I asked, pointing to the old crone I had bet with earlier. "My associate, a half-orc, made a bet with her earlier. Go get our gold."

"What are you doing?" Spudgum whispered to me as the MaHizzle bandits walked off toward the old bag.

"You'll see," I whispered back.

When the bandits returned, they had a hefty sack of gold. After they handed it to me, I gave it to the dwarves. They tried to refuse it, but I said, "It's for your temple. The last time I was there, it was in rough shape. Oh, and tell Fumblegums I said hi."

Chapter 20

I didn't mind going with the bandit gang. They offered me safety from the drooling crowd of gamblers who sought after the reward placed on my head, and I figured I'd abandon them as soon as the first opportunity arose. Besides that, we were marching just east of Mound Doom, which gave me high hopes of reaching Neverspring, again. If lucky, I'd be there before Bub and Lar returned with their wives from Port Laudervale. I hoped that I would be kicking my feet up at the Palm Eye Finger Magic Shop before they walked through the door!

"Where are we going?" I asked SloDrizzle, the bandit who asked me to join them.

"Our leader, Dogg, wanted us to catch up with him and the

rest of the MaHizzles at an orc encampment they were planning to raid," he explained. "Our leader has a nose for finding where these horrible monsters gather."

"Sounds like a ranger," I commented, while stepping over a log. "Is that how Dogg got his name?"

"Actually, no," chimed in GoPizzle, another one of the gang. "He was raised by gnolls, in the bad parts of Sunkensod. They named him."

"You like killin' orcs, rogue?" LeWizzle asked.

"Who doesn't," I replied to the third bandit walking with me. "But the best thing is watching the looks on their faces after I've stolen their gold, and I'm about to get away."

"Dead faces are the only good orc faces," LeWizzle said, scowling. "With their eyes bugging out as they fall off the end of my blade!"

I held back a yawn at his remark. I hoped he wasn't one of those blowhards who would talk endlessly of his minor exploits. I was wrong. So, I'd just shake my head, once-in-a-while, raise an eyebrow in fake interest, or both if I wanted to feign shock. The whole time he jabbered, I pictured him wetting himself whenever an orc came within twenty feet. He ended his tale with how all the ladies like him.

"Ask him about his girlfriend that we never seem to meet," GoPizzle said, fighting back a laugh.

"She is real," LeWizzle harumphed. "She's a cleric in Daggerfoot. She's rich."

The other two laughed as we kept walking. "I think I smell smoke," SloDrizzle said. "I wonder if that's Dogg and the gang burning down the encampment."

"Probably," GoPizzle commented while sniffing the air. "Unless LeWizzle is breaking wind, again."

LeWizzle just grinned and said, "Nope. Not me. If it were, you would have heard it, loud and unclear!"

I could smell smoke, now. But I could tell it was much more than burning huts. I could smell the faintness of flesh cooking, too. "Well, something died and is burning," I commented.

"Knowing Dogg, it's either the orcs or our lunch," GoPizzle laughed.

"It doesn't smell like anything I'd eat," I added. "It smells odd."

"What, you don't like horse meat?" SloDrizzle said, stopping to look at me. "Because it's our favorite."

My anger swelled up in me. "You eat horses?! Why in the realms would you do that?"

SloDrizzle just grinned. "Because they are so trusting and easy to catch," he stated. "We steal them, ride them, then chop em' up and eat em'!"

"What? You've never had boiled horsey hoof?" GoPizzle laughed, smacking his lips. "The secret is leaving the shoe on, for flavor!"

I bit my tongue and kept walking, trying not to let them see that my blood was beginning to boil. If fate had brought me here tonight for a reason, I assumed it would be to rescue the horses from these dirtbags. It didn't take long until we saw the orange light of fires in the night sky above the trees. We also heard the sounds of battle. Screaming, clanging of swords, and even spells being cast.

As the four of us jogged up closer, we stepped over many a dead orc, and even a bandit or two. LeWizzle stopped at one and took a few of his things. "Well," he chuckled. "I don't think PoGuzzle's going to be needing his wedding band!"

As we got even closer to the burning encampment, I realized something. None of the orc's I had seen were wearing armor, just dirtied tunics and other rags. I found this quite odd for an orc encampment. When we entered the main area, we caught the last of the orcs being slaughtered by the House of MaHizzle. Sitting in the center of it all, was a bald man in full plate armor, sitting on top of a black stallion. He had no facial hair whatsoever and had a simple grin on his face that was almost unnerving.

"That's Dogg," SloDrizzle pointed out, waving at their leader. "He never says a word. He just points, and we kind of figure out what he wants."

It didn't take long to see what SloDrizzle was saying as one of the bandits walked up to Dogg with an elderly orc in a chokehold. With a slicing motion over his throat with his finger, the bandit twisted the orc's neck, then dropped him on the ground. The simple grin never wavered on their leader's face. Dogg then looked at us, waved all around us, and nodded. He then turned his horse, waved his hand in the air, and motioned forward.

About twenty or so bandits jumped on horses laden with sacks of goods, and they rode off into the night. "What was that all about?" I asked GoPizzle.

The bandit turned to me and pointed all around. "We're to find anything of value that's left, load them onto the remaining horses, and follow him to our next job. I hope there's a big reward for ending this orcish threat!"

"This doesn't look like an encampment," I stated. "All I see are the bodies of younger adults and the elderly. None of them are wearing armor. I think this was a farming village!"

The three bandits walked closer to me. "Village or encampment," LeWizzle said. "What's the difference? You getting soft on us, rogue?"

The three began circling me with their hands on the hilts of their swords. "I didn't like the look on your face when I mentioned eating horse meat," GoPizzle said with a sneer. "I don't think you have the stomach for this kind of work!"

"I don't rob the weak or the poor," I said, calmly. "That would make me a coward, like you three."

"Whoa, there, mister," LeWizzle shot back, with firelight reflecting in his eyes. "We're not yellow, just smart!"

"What," SloDrizzle laughed. "You think we need your skills? That's a hoot. But we do know you have that special coin, and I think Dogg will be happy to have that in his paws!"

LeWizzle stepped forward and stuck his hand out. "Just set it gently in my palm. I don't want it to get all bloody."

The other two withdrew their long swords and stepped a little closer. "Listen to our friend here, rogue," GoPizzle hissed. "You want what's going to happen to you next to be quick and merciful."

I held up both my hands to show I was not holding a weapon,

and then reached into a pocket slowly, and pulled out my Coin of Cheating. "Are you sure you don't want to just flip for it?" I said, sweat forming on my brow.

"Pardon me if we don't find that joke funny," LeWizzle said, stepping close to me. "Now, put the coin in my hand!"

I reluctantly moved my hand over his and dropped the coin. Everything seemed to move in slow motion, at that point. While all three of their eyes moved to the falling coin, I quickly pulled Magurk from its sheath and slashed at LeWizzle's arm. As my magically sharp dagger sliced his hand off at the wrist, I used my telekinesis and pulled the coin back to my hand!

"Aaah!" the bandit screamed out in pain. "My hand!"

I pushed the screaming fool over and ran with my Boots of Speeding fast enough to dive over a wagon and activate my Cloak of Blending. "Where did you go, rogue! Come out and fight!" SloDrizzle shouted.

"I saw him disappear!" GoPizzle yelled as they flanked either side of the wagon. "He's got some kind of magic making him invisible!"

SloDrizzle reached down and started throwing sand in my direction. Then, GoPizzle did the same. "There he is!" SloDrizzle shouted when the falling dirt gave away my outline.

I did a quick roll out the way, but not fast enough. One of their swords slashed me across my back shoulder, slicing it open and shorting out the magic of my cloak. When I rolled back to face them, I hurled Magurk at SloDrizzle, and it embedded itself deep in his chest. Blood shot out of his mouth, and he sank to his knees. GoPizzle hesitated for a moment, then pulled the short bow off his back and tried to notch an arrow. I used this opportunity to run as fast as I could to find cover.

Lucky for me, I happened to see the horse pen. An arrow sailed past my face, striking a post. I know I could have run off at this point, but I wasn't about to leave the horses in the hands of these lunatics! I jumped the fence and hid behind a trough of water. As I caught my breath, I felt a nuzzle from one side of me. I turned to see the horse and couldn't believe my eyes. "Encumbrance!" I said. "My friend!"

Encumbrance was the horse I traveled with from time to time. Most people assume that I own her, but that is never the case. I let her roam free, and that's precisely what she does. I hadn't seen her in a while, so I assumed she was off having a good time. I had no idea bandits had captured her! The mere thought of Encumbrance as a main dish for GoPizzle infuriated me and gave me a burst of adrenaline. When I heard an arrow hit the trough, I jumped up and pulled the Swatfly bow off my back.

GoPizzle saw me and struggled to notch another arrow, but it was too late. I aimed and launched an arrow hitting him square in the gut. He cried out in pain, dropped his weapon, and writhed in the dirt. I patted Encumbrance on the head and gave her neck a quick hug. I opened up the pen right after that and let all the horses go. "My horses," GoPizzle groaned from the ground.

"Now you don't have to worry about eating them," I stated, kneeling next to him. "I doubt you have the stomach for it, anymore."

GoPizzle gurgled something incoherent before I stood up and walked back over to SloDrizzle's body to retrieve my dagger. I pulled it out of his motionless chest, wiped it clean on his hair, then pushed him over onto the ground. With a quick search of his body, I pulled out a Potion of Healing. It was a much-needed item for my shoulder wound. I was just about to pop the cork when I heard a female scream!

"LeWizzle!" I stated, realizing that he might still be alive.

I ran to where I cut his hand off and couldn't see his corpse anywhere. Thanks to the firelight of the burning village, I could see a blood trail that led to a hut that was still intact. With Magurk in hand, I ran over and kicked in the flimsy door. Standing behind a female orc with a pregnant belly was LeWizzle. He had a pistol bow aimed at her. He was incredibly pale from the loss of blood.

"Stay back, rogue! Or she gets it, you understand?!" he screamed hoarsely. "You traitor!"

"Don't do it!" I warned him. "She's with child!"

"So what," he weakly laughed. "They are the evil ones!"

"Not from what I've seen tonight," I said in a calming tone. "Let's let bygones be bygones."

LeWizzle swooned a little, then shook his head to wake himself. "Listen," I tried again. "Let's just get her back on her bed, and we'll go get some gold."

"I can't," LeWizzle cried out. "Look what you did!"

He held up his still bleeding stump and blood shot out on the wall. "It's not a problem," I said, "I'll give you a hand!"

"But you're the one who took it…" LeWizzle mumbled before passing out and crumpling to the floor.

I quickly ran over and caught the female orc before she passed out. I laid her on the bed as gently as I could. I wanted to get out of there quickly to get Encumbrance and finish my mission. "Thank you," the orc said, grabbing my wrist.

"It's no problem," I replied. "Sorry about these scumbags destroying your village."

"You not one of them," she replied, in fairly good common. "You good human."

"That's up for debate," I said while looking at the door.

"It my time," she said through heavy breaths. "Do not go."

"Oh, you'll be fine," I said softly. "You're just a little bruised."

"No," she replied. "It…my…time!"

She looked at her belly, and then I did, too. My heart dropped into my stomach as I realized what she was asking of me. "Wait. What? Whoa!" I blurted out. "Listen, miss. I'm no cleric; I don't know how to do that stuff!"

She howled out in pain and started taking deeper breaths. "Please, human! Help me!"

With a deep breath, I lifted my head back, ignoring the pain in my shoulder. "Okay," I said. "I'm here for you."

A short time later, I held the crying infant and handed it to the mother. I could not believe what had just happened, and to this day, I have no words to describe it. So, I won't. I sat and chatted with the new mother for a while and gave her the healing potion that I had scrounged off SloDrizzle's body. When I was confident that she would be okay, I started to say goodbye. She grabbed my wrist, again, and pulled me close to her and the baby. "Not all orcs are bad," she told me.

"And not all humans are good," I replied, giving her a warm smile. "Make sure you protect that little guy."

"What is your name," she asked me.

"They call me Gwai Lo, or the Ghost man," I said.

"No," she said. "Your real name."

I leaned over and whispered it into her ear. "That a good name," she said. "I give my son your name."

I reached down and patted the baby's head, then took her hand and squeezed it. "Thank you," I said. "Maybe I'll come back someday to check on him."

As I walked to the door, she said, "What is this?"

She opened up her palm and showed me the Coin of Cheating. "Well," I said. "The kid is going to need things. That'll help you get them."

After leaving the hut, I felt different, like a great weight had been lifted from my shoulders. "Must be the blood loss," I mumbled.

I found Encumbrance waiting for me outside. The poor horse looked underfed, but had found a fair bit of grass to chew on. I rubbed her mane for a few minutes and let her eat. I sat down on the ground next to her and looked up at all the stars in the sky. It was incredibly bright that night, and for a moment, I just soaked in its beauty. I wondered what was up there, then realized I was on my back and falling asleep.

Encumbrance nudged me, and I snapped back out of it. I slowly stood back up and walked her to the horse pen area. The amount of blood I lost from my back wound had me feeling weak. I found just enough strength to put a saddle on Encumbrance and climb onto her back. As we left, I noticed the bloodied spot on the ground where GoPizzle used to be. Hopefully, he crawled off and died, but I knew I was in no shape to go looking him.

I leaned forward in the saddle and weakly mumbled "Fumble-gums," into Encumbrance's ear.

The horse walked on and on as we made our way toward Ne-verspring, slow but steady. She must have known the shape I was in, because I would fall in and out of consciousness. Then, I sensed something, and I woke up a little to hear a familiar and unwelcom-ing voice. "Well, well, well," it began. "Look what just arrived, On-quay."

At this point, I started to pass out. All that I heard was On-quay's voice saying, "Elfalfuh's going to love this. Search him for that special coin of his."

They came forward a little, then paused, probably to admire my suffering. "Looks like the low-life bit off more than he could chew," Apichat chuckled.

"What, like your barber?" I replied, slurring a bit, with an un-steady smirk. "I'd say that's pretty good for a donkey!"

"I hope you'll have that same smile when I present your head to Elfalfuh," Onquay cut in. "That is, if I don't rip it off with my bare hands, first!"

"I've seen you eat," I mumbled. "So I'm not surprised."

The last words I heard before passing out were Onquay stat-ing, "Watch out, you dumb horse!"

Chapter 21

When I woke up, I was in a comfortable bed with all my gear stacked neatly on a table next to me. "Fumblegums," I said, realiz-ing who was sitting next to me.

"Thank goodneth," he said. "I thawt you were going to thleep all day!"

"Where am I?" I said, sitting up.

My back pain was gone entirely, and I was feeling better than ever. I ran my hand over my sliced open tunic and touched the healed area of my skin. "Ith good to have you back," he chirped, happily.

"How did I get here?" I asked. "The last thing I remember was being surrounded by Apichat and Onquay, a couple of Elfalfuh's

159

thugs."

"Oh, thath easy," Fumblegums began to explain. "Hey, fel-lath!"

I heard a commotion outside the door, and then it opened. To my surprise, it was the two fat dwarves, Spudgum and Tate! "Good to have you back with us," Spudgum stated. "We healed you just in time!"

Tate nodded in agreement while brushing crumbs off his food-stained robe. "You were in horrible shape. It's a good thing your horse was protecting you."

"Encumbrance?" I said, sitting up. "Where is she, is she hurt?"

The two dwarves chuckled. "No, she's not hurt," Tate laughed. "But I wouldn't say the same thing about those two rogues who were trying to get you!"

"Yeah," Spudgum laughed. "The big, pale-looking one was clutching his chest when we arrived. She must have kicked him good!"

"The thin, slimy-looking one almost got to you," Spudgum stated. "But I laid him flat with my Ghost Hammer spell. He staggered off, hunched over, after where I hit him!"

The two dwarves laughed and high-fived one another. "What were you two doing there?" I asked. "I thought you were back in Neverspring already."

"Traveling is slow when you are packing this kind of muscle," Spudgum explained, patting his ample belly. "Plus, we had the large bag of gold you gave us."

"That stuff is killer on your back," Tate added. "It's a good thing I dabble in Chiromagic!"

"You see," Spudgum continued. "We were at our campsite last night, enjoying a wee nibble or two, when we heard a horse neighing and some laughter. When we went over to investigate, we saw Encumbrance kicking at the two thugs, keeping them away from you."

I smiled at the thought of Onquay getting a good kick from the horse. Just the thought of his broken ribs brought a warm, fuzzy feeling to my heart. "That's my girl," I bragged. "Where is she

160

now?"

"Sheeth in the temple thtable, getting fed and refrethed," Fumblegums stated happily. "By the way, the head cleric wanth to talk to you before you go."

After the three clerics left, I put on my gear and checked my pockets, especially the hidden ones, to see if I was missing anything. They hadn't touched a thing. I did note a few things were added, though. Next to my poison vials on my bandolier were three blue vials that were labeled Healing Potions.

That's when I noticed my Cloak of Blending was missing. Frantically, I searched under the bed and all around the room. It had been damaged and shorted out, but I knew it could be repaired. I figured I'd have Bub and Lar look at it a few days after their return, so that they wouldn't get suspicious. My blood pressure was starting to rise, the more I thought about it. Fumblegums probably removed it, sneezed in it a few times, and wiped his nose before throwing it into a rubbish bin!

"Looking for something," a voice came from the doorway of the room, which I wasn't facing.

When I turned around, the head cleric of the Gallowman Temple was standing there with my cloak, draped neatly over one arm. "Glad to see you survived!" he commented.

"I'm glad to see my cloak," I said, as he passed it to me. "And it's fixed!"

"It's the least we could do," the cleric said. "Especially after you tried to save our temple, twice!"

I was utterly puzzled by this statement, but nodded back, as if I knew what he was talking about. "Well," I said. "It wasn't much."

"Exposing the Undead Poet Society and ruining their plans of a coordinated attack," he marveled. "That was pure genius!"

"Well, someone had to do it," I fibbed. "I'm a real people person. Well, as long as they're alive."

"Then, you rescued Spudgum and Tate," the cleric continued. "And then gave them gold to help rebuild parts of the temple. You, sir, are a role model!"

"That's me," I lied. "I get that a lot!"

I put on the cloak and tested it, disappearing for a moment, then deactivated it. "Nice," I commented.

"We have a Magechanic on staff, and he fixed it right up," the head cleric stated. "It's one of the perks of having the largest temple in Neverspring."

"Do you mind looking after my friend, Encumbrance, for a while?" I asked. "I have somewhere I need to be at the moment, and I'm running out of time."

"That is not a problem," he replied. "Take your time. Oh, and when you come back, maybe you can explain how you discovered the Undead Poet Society and how you came up with such a great plan to expose them, especially when there would be so many clerics here to stop them!"

"Um, yeah," I replied. "But I'd just be afraid I'd bore you all to death with all that hero-y stuff."

The cleric just laughed, and we shook hands. "You're modest, too!"

I said a quick goodbye to Fumblegums, Spudgum, and Tate as I exited the temple. I figured I'd sneak back in later, break Encumbrance out, and then ride out to see Amberfawn, my faerie girlfriend. The last thing I wanted was to be squished between the two fat dwarves as the guest of honor as Fumblegums shouted my praises while gumming a mouth full of food.

I walked out of the Gallowman Temple and started running back toward the Palm Eye Finger Magic Shop. With any luck, I would be there before Bub and Lar made their triumphant return. It was just about noon, and that's when they said they would be back. I had a lot of respect for the two old wizards, and I didn't want them to think I took my security position lightly.

* * *

Chapter 22

It was a busy day in Neverspring, and people were moving through the streets doing their daily business. At some points, the congestion was so bad that I had to slow down to a walk, so that I wouldn't trip over anyone. That was okay, though; it gave me a reason to be in close enough quarters to pick a few pockets. I couldn't get near the street vendors; they watched me like a hawk. I do think that is unfair, though, because I hadn't stolen anything from them... yet. For now, I just picked a few of their customer's pockets. I even acquired a lovely gem-encrusted pocket sundial off one.

I ran down the street until I spotted the shop that I was supposed to be guarding. I ran up to its side and looked in the windows. I sighed with relief as I could see the lights were still off. When I walked around the corner to the front door, it was a whole other story. Lying on the ground in front of the door was Schmendrake the Mage.

The wizard looked to be in rough shape. For a moment, I wondered why some citizen of Neverspring didn't come to his aid, but then it hit me, the smell. It was a strong odor of unwashed feet, skunk, and cattle's business. Schmendrake didn't look too well, either. His face was all blackened from some kind of smoke and his hair was burnt off. Plus, he looked as though a giant had sneezed on him. When he saw me, he slowly sat up, with green globs of goo dripping off of him.

"What happened to you?" I asked.

"How many traps did they put on this place?" Schmendrake asked blearily. "One day, it's pies hitting you in the face, and the next, it's prankenfairies dumping magic manure!"

"How long have you been here?" I asked, seeing signs of other traps that had been set off. "Because it looks like you've been hit with everything in their arsenal!"

"I've been here every night since you've been gone," he sighed. "I never knew what each night would bring, either a teleporting bucket of giant snot or fiery arrows to the backside!"

On wobbly legs, he stood up and grinned at me while straightening out his glasses. A multi-cracked lens almost completely hid his one eye. Schmendrake then pointed at me and laughed. "But I got you to stay away by putting a curse on you and your coin! I bet you're still trying to find it!"

So, that's the reason why I couldn't keep it in my possession! It all made sense to me, now. Still, I didn't let my emotions about it show.

"Actually," I said. "I gave it away."

"What!?" Schmendrake screamed. "But the curse only works when you're trying to keep it! It doesn't work on anybody else! Didn't a bunch of bad stuff happen to you?!"

"Nothing major," I lied. "I just chased it a bit, then gave it away. You know how it is. Now, if you'll excuse me, I have to get into the shop."

I waved him aside, lifted the welcome mat, and picked up the key where I had hidden it. "Are you kidding me?!" the wizard yelled, pulling at the last tuft of hair remaining on his head. "I can't believe it!"

"By the way," I said, noticing his shop down the street. "I think your shop got robbed. I can see the broken front window. It must have happened while you were here."

"Argh!" Schmendrake screamed when noticing it, as well.

I watched for a few seconds as the wizard hobbled down the street, yelling out things that I wouldn't repeat.

Then, I stepped into the Palm Eye Finger shop, clapped my hands twice, and the magical lights on the walls lit up. I strolled behind the counter and sat in one of the two chairs. Then, I grabbed a few bits of jerky they kept beside the register. I was still chewing my snack with my feet up on the counter when a swirling blue portal opened, and the two wizards stepped through, wearing colorful flowered shirts.

"You two came back just in time," I cheerfully stated. "I was starting to get bored!"

The older men laughed joyfully and wandered over. Bub waved his hand shooing my feet off the counter. "The wives wanted to stay another couple of days," he declared. "But Lar and I can't be away from the shop that long; we started going crazy!"

"Port Laudervale is quite lovely this time of year," Lar stated. "Even though it was flooded with guild students from all over the realms."

"Thankfully, we know a teleport spell," Bub said, while unpacking a few baubles from a bag he was carrying. "Because the lairports were packed."

"Wow," I said, moving out of their way.

"Not only that," Lar said. "There's some scuttlebutt going around that a green dragon crashed into the Barrendry desert!"

"Really," I said, pretending to be stunned. "That's horrible."

"That's why I won't fly on one of those creatures," Bub said, pittering around the shop. "They say it's the safest way to travel, but you always hear about a crash or someone being eaten. I tell you, it's just not for me."

"Did the wives have fun?" I asked.

"We couldn't get them out of the Brown Cushion Tavern last night," Lar said when unpacking a few spell components. "They went all googoo for the lead lute player in some band with a crazy lizard singer."

"I've heard of them," I remarked. "The drummer seems cool."

"It's a good thing the food upset all our stomachs," Lar stated. "Or we would have never left!"

"No need to go into details on that," I asserted. "I haven't had a proper lunch."

"So, did we miss anything?" Bub asked.

I thought about what to say for a minute, then replied. "It was quiet here," I said, being as honest as possible.

As a gift, I gave them both the golden pocket sundial that I had acquired. The two mages immediately began to think of ways to enhance it magically and started chattering on in their wizardly-jargon. Before I could leave, they gave me an Orbiting Stone shaped like a red diamond. "It's our latest invention," Bub remarked. "We made it just for you."

"What does it do?" I asked.

Lar grinned widely. "You're going to love this," he said, pulling out a deck of cards and dealing them out.

"Watch this," he said, as he picked up the gem and tossed it up by his head.

It immediately disappeared. "That's neat, so what?" I said,

wondering what they were up to.

"Pick up your cards," Bub stated, staring at my hand. "Go ahead."

When I picked them up, Lar immediately told me each one. "2 of spades, 6 of hearts, queen of clubs, 7 of clubs, and finally, a jack of diamonds!"

"How did you know that?" I said, amazed.

The wizards both laughed and gave each other a fist bump. "Well," Bub explained. "I put a spell on the gem, making it invisible whenever in use. Then, Lar put a slight mind-reading spell on it. The moment your brain recognized the cards, he saw an image of that in his mind."

"It's a way to cheat at cards telepathically," Lar beamed proudly. "We thought you might get a kick out of it."

I was stunned and happy. "This is the coolest gift I've not stolen," I said gleefully before, turning toward the front door. "I appreciate the thoughtful gesture. If you need me again, I'll be around."

"Where are you headed?" Bub asked.

"To Miftenmad," I answered. "I want to see about challenging the Black Willow gang to a game of cards at the Dice Tower Tavern."

"Wait!" Lar shouted, jumping up from his seat. "I almost forgot to give you this!"

The balding mage ran over and placed a small piece of paper into my hand. "What's this?" I asked.

"Instructions," he replied. "Follow these few steps, and you'll have this working in no time. Just don't lose them, I only wrote one copy."

I put the small slip of paper into the same pocket with the little gem. "Thanks," I said. "Today is going to be my lucky day."

I walked out of the Palm Eye Finger Magic Shop feeling pretty good. The two wizards were happy, and so was I. Plus, I had a new way to cheat and make money, again! I decided to take a look at my latest treasure. When I pulled the red diamond out, the little instruction slip came out with it. To my dismay, it slipped out of my

166

grasp and was picked up by a sudden gust of wind. Frustrated, I started to run after it, but the wind picked up more, and it started flying faster and higher, moving farther and farther away.

I thought about going back to the wizards for a new one, but I didn't want them to perceive me as an imbecile who would lose their thoughtful gift's instructions so quickly. I thought I could reach it, so I ran as fast as I could and jumped! Unfortunately, I didn't see the overweight eleven woman who had just walked into the way. I crashed down and hit the ground hard. I looked over at her just as I heard her say, "You! I know you!"

It was the same lady I crashed into earlier that week and had seen at the lairport! "Stop, thief!" she yelled, pointing at me.

The crowd around us stopped what they were doing and looked at me angrily before starting to come my way. I jumped to my feet and spotted my slip of paper flittering away in the wind. Just beneath it was a halfling who must have spotted me chasing it and was now pursuing it, as well. "Robbie!" I growled, realizing who it was.

The little guy ran fast, then magically jumped high into the air and grabbed my slip of paper! It was Schmendrake's Magic Boots of Jumping! So, he was the one who had broken into the idiotic wizard's shop! Even though Robbie could jump high and far, I had my Boots of Speeding, and I was gaining fast. The problem was that there was a large crowd chasing me, as well!

Eventually, I caught up with the runt, and we made a deal. But not before a long chase that had taken us both all over the realms. But that story, dear reader, is an entry for another day.

EPILOGUE

As an older man, I still enjoyed going to the Dice Tower Tavern to play a board game and maybe do a little gambling. One particular day, I sat down across from a hooded orc who was counting cards on a table. "Care for a game?" I asked.

His smile grew from under the cowl he wore. I assumed he was a fellow rogue and was keeping a low profile, just like I liked to do. "Got any gold?" I asked.

"Some," he replied, in amazingly good common.

"Not for long," I said, cracking my knuckles.

He just laughed and started dealing the cards. "What's your name, kid?" I asked as I peeked at his hand.

Little did he know, I already knew what cards he was holding. I could feel the slight breeze from the invisible diamond circling my head. "I never give out my name," he replied. "My mother said it is special and one of good fortune."

"Mine, too," I said, checking out my cards. "No point in making yourself easily trackable."

Over the next couple of hours, we had a good time, mostly by calling out each other's cheating maneuvers. By the end of the night, I felt tired; I wasn't able to stay up as late as I used to, so I decided to say goodbye to this interesting fellow. "Why don't you stay a bit longer," the orc asked. "We're all evened up. We should have a tiebreaker."

"I'm too tired," I yawned. "We had our fun."

"C'mon, how bout we flip a coin for winner-take-all?" he asked, pulling out a coin.

It wasn't just any coin; it was my coin. My precious Coin of Cheating! I watched him flip the coin a few times in the air while he waited for my response. The desire to get my coin back was strong, but I was honestly just happy to see the kid had done all right. "Naw," I said, laying a few gold pieces on the table. "I have to go; my bladder isn't what it used to be!"

"You don't trust me, rogue?" he said, smiling. "I promise on this very coin that the toss will be fair. You can trust me; not all orcs are bad."

"True. But not all humans are good," I replied, before bending down and wishing him good luck into his ear, along with his name.

"That is my mother's favorite saying," he said in a hushed tone.

He looked at the coin, then at me, and grinned. I smiled back. "Best of luck, kid. It was nice seeing you, again."

I turned and left before he could say anything else. It was for the best. Besides, I didn't want to keep my wife waiting at home. It's never a good thing to keep a tooth faerie waiting up. As I waved goodnight to Vasel, Jr., the Dice Tower Tavern owner, I turned to see the kid writing down something in a journal that looked a lot like one of the ones I'd usually carry.

Featured Artist
Josh Will

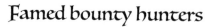

Famed bounty hunters
Sunshine & Moonbeam

See more of Josh's great art at: www.joshwill.com

Josh Will

Chook

Hauk

HeeHaw

Skole

Tuddle

Pacoyma

Quade

Infamous dwarven gang

The Black Willows

See more of Josh's great art at: www.joshwill.com

Back when I was 8 years old I bought a game from my local Ben Franklin store. The game was called Dwarf Mountain and it was from Grenadier Model Company. Little did I know that it would have such a big impact on my life. I was mesmerized by the Dwarves on the cover fighting a dragonlike snake. My 12 year old uncle figured out how to play it and it opened my eyes to a new fantasy world. Later, I moved on to Dungeons & Dragons and others but I always remembered that game.

To my delight, I was able to find this rare game on eBay and was able to purchase it. As I admired the artwork once again, more than 40 years later, I wondered who the artist was. Through a bit of detective work I found a name, Martin Kealey. Luckily, I was able to find his contact information and talk to him. He is still creating artwork to this day, and I am thrilled to show a piece of his work here, that he created special for the book series.

I would have had him draw the Outlaw, but I figured that since the first work I saw of his was dwarves, I thought I'd have him do a take on Badwigg the Cleric, one of Outlaw's many traveling companions. I want to say thank you to Martin for doing this, because his drawing style brings a lot of joy to me and it's awesome to have his image as part of the Unremembered Realms!

Martin Kealey

Badwigg the Dwarven Cleric

The Rogues Gallery

I would like to thank these fellow adventurers who, in one way or another, have decided to journey with the Outlaw. These scoundrels have been a boon in making the Unremembered Realms grow. Their support has helped make these stories a success!

Nonie Osantowski

Javier A Verdin

Daniel Edwards

Twyste

Clickot

Richard Ohnemus

Ian Holmer

Tniu

Abe, Asher, Max, and Aaron Jager

Steven Callen

Josh Will

Steve McEntire

Dan the Man

Terri the Terrible

John "AcesofDeath7" Mullens

Greg Tausch

Esapekka Eriksson

Steve Jones

Cote Voskuhl

Matt Mueller

Judy

Samantha Roderick

Chloe

Eric Waydick

Charles Vass

Journee G

THE
UNREMEMBERED
REALMS

Also available from the Unremembered Realms:
Books:
Journal of an Outlaw: Books 1, 2, & 3
Journal of an Awful Good Paladin: Book 1

Games & Accessories:
The Forbidden Treasure of Miftenmad
The Fumblecrit Wars
Gamble at the Gallows
Merch Madness
Die of Destiny
The Naughty Dice Jail

Music:
Scales & The Marshtones "Found on the Road" CD

Coming Soon:
Journal of an Awful Good Paladin: Book 2
Journal of a Lounge Lizardman: Book 1
The Game Rooms Throne Game

T-shirts & other merch now available on the website

Make sure to check the website for
Mick's book signing schedule.

Join the email list for product updates
and book signing locations!
www.unrememberedrealms.com
and fill out a short sign-up form.

THIS BOOK IS INDEPENDENTLY PUBLISHED,
IT WOULD BE A HUGE HELP TO THE AUTHOR
IF YOU COULD PLEASE TAKE A MOMENT
AND REVIEW THIS BOOK ON YOUR
FAVORITE BOOK SITE LIKE AMAZON.COM,
GOODREADS.COM, OR AUDIBLE.COM.
PLEASE GIVE THIS BOOK SERIES
A MENTION ON YOUR FAVORITE
SOCIAL MEDIA AS WELL.

STAY UP TO DATE WITH THE OUTLAW
BY JOINING THE
UNREMEMBERED REALMS
MAILING LIST!
GO TO
UNREMEMBEREDREALMS.COM
AND FILL OUT THE SHORT
FORM ON ANY OF THE PAGES!

ABOUT THE AUTHOR

Mick McArt is the author of the "Journal of an Outlaw" comedy fantasy book series which takes place in the Unremembered Realms. The other two series are Journal of an Awful Good Paladin and Journal of a Lounge Lizardman. Mick is also an illustrator and author of children's books, his most popular being the "Tales of Wordishure" series.

Mick is a full-time Multimedia Designer that is currently running his own multimedia company, Mick Art Productions. Thanks to a growing fan base on Kickstarter, Mick has also become a game designer, with a number of games being composed based on the Unremembered Realms.

Currently, Mick is working on a Homeschool Art Curriculum for all ages and a role playing system for the Unremembered Realms. Micks family include his wife Erica, and their children Micah, Jonah, and Emerald.

Mick earned a Bachelor of Fine Arts degree from Central Michigan University in 1997 and a Masters degree from Saginaw Valley State University in 2006.

Made in the USA
Middletown, DE
01 August 2022

70309420R00106